Jack Be Nimble

JACK
BE
NIMBLE

A NOVEL

by George Cuomo

Doubleday & Company, Inc.
Garden City, New York
1963

All of the characters in this book
are fictitious, and any resemblance
to actual persons, living or dead,
is purely coincidental.

For Sylvia

Nimble: From Middle English *nimmel;*
Anglo-Saxon *numol,* from *niman,*
to take, catch, seize; basic
sense "capable of taking,"
"quick at taking"; becomes *to nim,*
to take, especially to steal, hence
nimmer, a thief; also in compounds
scearp-numul, literally "sharp taking,"
and *teart-numul,* literally "tart taking."

Jack Be Nimble

CHAPTER ONE

The accident, which as we said in the *Standard* the next morning, narrowly missed being a real tragedy, seemed at the moment of its occurrence marvelously comical, almost hilarious. I was standing behind the bench when the kid sort of exploded into the air, his arms and legs flailing like broken sticks, his head swirling, looping, as if attached to his body by a string. He turned a somersault in the air and landed on his back like an ironing board, his head snapping. Dancer had gone sailing through low—hitting the kid right at the knees—so hard that he had slid fifteen or twenty feet past the kid on the grass.

It had been a typical play for Dancer. Pug, who didn't want to take a chance on Dancer getting hurt in a scrimmage, had just sent him in a few minutes before to let him loosen up a bit. He had taken a punt on his own fifteen and had moved to about the fifty, not even running very fast or trying hard, just sliding past the tacklers, and then had shifted into that beautiful high gear of his and cut for the sidelines. He sprinted down to about the thirty before someone from the secondary boxed him in, and then he tried for a few extra yards by diving forward and out—not even noticing the kids standing along the sideline watching. The one he hit flipped up like a tiddlywink.

Pug, desperate, frightened, was the first one over. He ran past the kid and grabbed Dancer, who was still face down on the grass. "You all right, Dan? You all right?"

He was. He got up, brushed himself, shrugged his shoulder pads into place.

"You sure now?" Pug held his arms, not letting him move. But Dancer looked fine; Pug was the one shaken up.

"Yeah," Dan said, pulling away. "I'm all right. I'm fine."

Pug nodded and let him walk away. His tongue moved over his lips. He took a full breath and looked around him, as if suddenly realizing there was still a world there. He went over to look at the kid, who was still out, flat on his back, with a bunch of the players around him.

"Is he hurt?" Pug asked, his face expressionless now, as he moved the padded hulks aside with a touch, the touch of someone used to handling men bigger than himself. He stared down at the kid.

Phil Lichey, the trainer, sponged the kid's face and his eyes snapped open. He saw everyone looking at him from above. He sat up abruptly. "Lemme go." He jumped to his feet and started running, with the players scrambling out of his way, but made only about five steps before his legs jellied and he tipped over again, face down.

"Get someone to take him home," Pug said. "And keep those damn kids out of the way."

Pug put Dancer back on the bench and kept him there the rest of the scrimmage. The second team beat the varsity 14–6. Pug was not very happy with the way anybody looked.

I was heading for the locker room when I saw Andy Rivers coming along the cinder track. I pretended not to see him and gradually slanted out of his path, walking a little faster, my chin stiff and my features hardening into that purposeful expression Andy favored for his campus correspondents.

"Jack," he called. He had a thin, unmistakable, penetrating voice, but I was so intent upon my assignment that he had to call again before I heard him.

"Oh," I said. "Hello." I slanted back to him. He took out his handkerchief and wiped his face. He would sweat sitting on a cake of ice. He was short and pretty fat—not tremendously, but soft and pudgy all over—and he was winded from walking. If fifty years from now I tried to remember Andy Rivers I'd probably forget everything, even the comb-and-toilet-paper voice, but I'd remember him sweating and trying to catch his breath.

I gave him a pack of Lords. "Have some smokes, Mr. Rivers."

He grunted and stuck them in his pocket. Everybody always looked as if they were doing you a favor, but they always took them.

"You're going out with Dancer," he said. "Take the camera, get some good shots."

"Yes, Mr. Rivers. Out where?"

"To see that kid. In the hospital, wherever the hell he is. Get Dancer autographing his cast or something."

"Did he break his leg?"

"I don't know. Find out."

"Maybe I can get him autographing a football—if the kid didn't break anything, I mean."

"Okay. Pug's going too. Get them all in."

"When they leaving?"

"Find out. Get it in early tonight for a change, okay?"

"Yes, sir."

I found Pug in his office in the catacombs under the gym. I dropped a pack of Lords on his desk and asked him when we were going.

"I don't know. Right away, I guess. The kid's at home."

The whole thing, naturally, was Andy Rivers' idea. Pug wasn't much for public relations.

"Where's Dancer?" I asked.

"He hadda call somebody. He had something else on."

"You mean he had a date?"

"I don't know. He wouldn't say."

I heard the little moan in his voice, but for some reason didn't pay much attention to it. You spend your whole life looking for the little breaks, the little openings you can squeeze through. You get very skillful at finding them in the unlikeliest places. Then someone really throws the gates open for you and you don't even notice; you have to be pushed through.

"I'll go get him," I said, and headed down the hall to the phone. Dancer was coming out of the booth.

"Hi," I said. He sure looked different in clothes. In uniform he looked more like a football player—like a half-back, I should say—than anyone I've ever seen. He looked like George Gipp, Doak Walker, Frank Gifford. But in regular clothes, even only the slacks and sport shirt he wore now, he looked like an artist, a bullfighter, a dancer; he looked like the pampered scion of some family with a nine-hundred-year-old name, like the young lawyer just lured away from the best law firm in town by the best law firm in New York.

"You finished with the phone?"

He nodded. He wasn't much of a talker.

I stepped in and dialed Peggy.

"Sorry, kid, but I won't be able to make it for the soirée tonight. I gotta go out on a story and then I gotta write it up and take it downtown. Probably be hung up until eight, nine o'clock, at least."

"I don't think Daddy'll last until eight."

"Let's make it tomorrow, then."

"He's all set for tonight."

"A newsman is a slave to the news," I informed her. "Through the ages, newsmen have been unsuccessful in scheduling events conveniently—earthquakes, wars, fires, floods . . ."

"Hold on. I'll ask Daddy."

I held on.

"He said come then."

"When?"

"Eight o'clock. He's really all set for it."

"All right. Go ahead and eat though. I don't want him on my hands with an empty stomach."

"I hope it all comes out all right," she said.

"It'll come out fine," I assured her. "Trust me."

We rode out in Pug's Chevy, which was five years old and not very classy. Maybe he was sensitive about being the highest-paid man on campus, or waiting for his first winning year, when the Townbirds would probably give him a new Caddy. Pug drove and I sat in the middle with the camera and a new football on my lap. Dancer sat at the window, looking out. No one said much, and I used the time to write out the story in my head. My best stories were always worked out beforehand. Sports writing lends itself to that sort of thing.

"Was the kid hurt bad?" I asked Pug.

"No."

"Didn't he break an arm or a leg or anything?"

"No."

"What about a concussion? He was out for a while and maybe—"

"Phil said he seemed all right. Just a little dizzy for a while."

I changed the story around a bit. Dancer was still gazing out at the houses and the trees along the street. Midland was really a nice place—especially in summer. The students were coming back, though, and the little town of fifty thousand would face another nine-month siege of its yearly, and always near fatal, disease. But now it was still quiet and sunny, and everything looked pretty good.

When we pulled up to the kid's house I made a few more revisions in the story. It was quite a house.

"Hey—who is this kid anyhow?"

"Father's Sam Rending," Pug said. "They got dough."

"What's he do?"

"Contractor. But he won't give you any trouble. He's in with the Birds."

The Townbirds were the local fan group, businessmen mostly. A tenth of them never got over having once played football, and the other nine tenths never got over having never played football. They had been pretty rough on Pug the year before, and Pug despised them. Although, of course, he was always nice to them. They could help a coach a lot, if they weren't out to get him. At the moment, the Birds were trying to decide which they wanted to do with Pug.

I knocked at the door and a colored maid let us in. The kid's mother was older than I expected with such a young kid, and pretty bitchy.

"If you don't mind, I'd rather you let him alone. You'll get him all excited again."

"But ma'am—Coach Walters and Mr. Danciewitz just want to say hello. I'm sure it'll be quite a thrill for the little boy, meeting a couple of his heroes."

"He hates football."

"But he came over to watch."

"His friends dragged him there. I've made him promise never to do it again."

"But maybe he was enjoying it."

"He could get killed there for all you people cared."

"Is Mr. Rending by any chance at home?"

"Mr. Rending takes care of his business, and I take care of raising our children."

"A fine arrangement, I'm sure. Here, would you like a pack of Lords? Well—I'll just leave them on the table. I thought, though, that since your husband is such an ardent athletic—"

"I'm not really concerned with his hobbies."

I wasn't getting much help from my friends. Pug stared at the lady like she was the barber pole and he was waiting his turn. Dancer was looking out the window. He was a great one for windows.

"Maybe if you'd just let us go upstairs and ask your son if he'd—"

"He's not upstairs."

"Isn't he in bed?"

"He's out playing. But I won't have you talking to him behind my back."

"Of course not. Couldn't we just give him the football we brought him?"

"I told you, he hates football. He's not a strong boy and he doesn't like sports."

"Mr. Danciewitz was also once a very fragile child. Perhaps your son would be inspired to meet a great athlete who overcame—"

"I don't think he would."

Pug was getting restless and started giving me high signs toward the door when it opened and the kid walked in.

"Who are they?" he demanded of his mother. He really wasn't very sturdy looking.

"Some men who were just leaving, dear."

"How'd you like to have your picture in the paper tomorrow?" I asked him.

"I don't know," he said.

"I think you'd better leave," the mother told us.

"It won't hurt him any. He'd enjoy it."

"Enjoy what?"

"Having your picture taken with Dancer and Coach Walters."

"Who?"

"Coach Walters is our football coach at the University. Dancer here is our star halfback."

The kid examined them.

"Dancer is the player who accidentally bumped into you today. He came to say hello, to tell you he was sorry. He wants to autograph this football for you. Wouldn't you like that?"

The kid stared at Dancer, who was still pretty much looking out the window.

"You can say hello to—what *is* your name, sonny?"

"Timmy."

"—to Timmy."

"Hello," Dancer said. He had a marvelous voice: crisp, clear, pleasant. "Sorry I had to go into you . . . Hope you're okay."

Timmy shrugged. "I'm okay. Can I have the football now?"

"Wouldn't you like Dancer to autograph it for you?"

"I guess so."

"Well, c'mon, let's go up to your bed, then."

"His bed?" the mother said.

"Yes . . . I thought it'd look better if—"

"But he's not *in* bed. He doesn't have to be in bed. Why are you making everything phony?"

"We're not making anything phony, ma'am. Didn't he rest at all when he came home?"

"For about three minutes."

"And we just happened to miss him then. Now we'd simply like to recreate the—"

"All right, all right. Do what you want. Just get it over with."

We trooped upstairs. I got the kid to put on his pajamas and took a few shots with Dancer aiming a pen at the football while the kid gloated and Pug and the mother looked on. I angled the old lady out of the last few shots; she looked like Dancer was about to castrate the kid instead of giving him a goddamn football.

"My head hurts," the kid said.

The mother frowned, eying me accusingly. "You should lie down and rest. The excitement isn't good for you."

"That's right," I agreed. "You get plenty of rest now, sonny."

"Maybe we should call the doctor," the mother said.

"I don't want any doctor. My head just hurts."

"Well, you rest then, or I will call him."

We got out fast at this point; the kid was getting ideas from all the attention. The old lady was, too. Before you'd know it she'd be suing us for permanent brain damage or something.

I still had my story to write up, but Pug said he wanted to talk to me first. He dropped Dancer at his dorm and then we drove to his house.

CHAPTER TWO

"Have a pack of Lords, Pug."

"You gave me one before."

"Have another."

He took it. They always take them.

"Don't you ever run out of these things?"

"The well is bottomless," I said.

We were in his study. Caroline was out, and they didn't have any kids. The house was like the car—all right, but not what you'd expect with the money they were paying him. He sat at his desk, which was a mess of papers and stubby pencils and trophies. The walls were covered with those dreary, glossy, gray-brown football squads, four rows of stiff heads and zombied eyes, with an occasional smile and one man looking off in another direction. Pug himself didn't look much like a football player, or even an ex-football player. He was pretty small and didn't look strong, or quick, or graceful. But then you found out he played first-string guard for three years at Minnesota—at 145 pounds—and then you knew why he was a good coach, which he was. You could see him pleading with Bernie Bierman to give him a uniform, to let him on the field, you could see this kid who wasn't anything—not big, not strong, not fast—beating out guys who outweighed him by 80

pounds—and doing it for three years running. And then you
knew that when he spoke about guts and determination
that at least to him the clichés meant something. He once
said he'd like to bar from his squads anyone who weighed
over 200 pounds or who could run the 100 under twelve
seconds. They had too much in their favor; it'd be too easy
for them. He wanted only the ungraced and the unen-
dowed, the midgets, the punks, the oafs, because he knew
they'd work.

Pug didn't give many pep talks, about guts and determination or anything else, and he never yelled at anyone,
never raised his voice. He demanded a lot, though, and
he got it. The kids didn't mind working for him, because
he was straight and he knew his stuff. He came to us from
a line job at Mississippi, after Andy Rivers and the Townbirds hung the guy we had. Pug inherited a pretty weak
team. His first year was 2–6, but no one complained; no
one expected miracles right away. The second year they
did expect miracles, and Pug got some bad breaks and
ended up with another 2–6. He was starting his third year
now, on a three-year contract, and the Birds were growing
restless. At one time or another everything and everybody
got blamed for the team's showing—the governor, the legislature, the regents, President Irvine, the kids themselves,
the admission standards, the grading standards, the lack
of scholarships, the lack of school spirit, the lack of a
bigger stadium. The state labor-union paper got into the
act by blaming the big-money interests. The Midland
American Legion Post blamed left-wing professors. And the
owner of a grocery wrote a letter to the *Standard* blaming
the high schools for making the students read *Othello* and
a lot of obscene modern novels that nobody could understand instead of teaching the three Rs and keeping up the
state's reputation by producing good football material. But

Pug and everyone else knew that if the team floundered
again, all the guesswork would stop. It would be Pug's
fault, and he'd be finished.

Pug stuffed his pipe and lit it. All he ever smoked was
a pipe—one finger was always black from being used as a
tamper.

"Dan seem any different to you this year, Jack?"

"Not really," I said. Actually, I hadn't seen too much of
Dancer since he had come back.

"I don't know," Pug said. "I think he's changed."

"He does seem a little different."

Pug nodded. "Bored, or something. Listless, no zest.
Resentful, even. I can't talk to him any more. He never
says nothing."

"He was always kinda quiet."

"I don't know. He was a good kid last year. I liked him a
lot." He shook his head and was quiet for a moment. "You
got to know Dan pretty good last year, didn't you?"

"Pretty good," I said. Dancer had been in my tutoring
group, along with a couple of sophomore guards and two
junior tackles. I hit them three times a week in English
and history and things like that.

"You two got along okay, didn't you? I mean, Dan liked
you, didn't he?"

How had I missed those gates swinging open before?
"We got along great," I said. "Actually we're still pretty
much best friends. I mean, well, I don't know anybody on
campus I'd rather . . ."

Pug sucked on his pipe. "Were you figuring on Dan in
your group again?"

"Well, I *hoped* he would be in. He was making such
good progress, and we had gotten to be such good friends,
that—"

"All right." He chewed on his pipe some. He usually

worked through a stem in about a month. "I don't know," he said. "I'm worried about Dan this year."

"Well, if there's anything I can do . . ."

Pug waited a minute, working over the pipe. "We were thinking maybe you could drop the study group this season . . . just work with Dan."

"That sounds great."

"Good. Of course, Dan doesn't really need all that work . . . I mean, he actually did pretty well last year."

"He did fine," I said, with a lot more honest pride than Pug realized. My real achievement was not in simply getting Dancer through, but in getting people to believe he was at least partially responsible himself. Dancer was pretty slow, even for an athlete.

"We'd like you to kinda just keep an eye on things . . . you know, stay in touch with him. He's a funny egg, so quiet and everything. I don't know—maybe he's got mixed up with some broads or something. The girls go for him, don't they?"

"But he doesn't go near them. He hardly even goes out."

"Well, I don't want him getting into *any* kind of trouble—girls, grades, booze, anything."

"His grades are good, he stays away from girls, and he never drinks."

"You'll have it easy, then. And we'll feel better having someone a little older keeping an eye on him . . . How old are you, anyhow?"

"Twenty-five. I spent some time in the Navy."

"A junior?"

"A senior, more or less."

He nodded. "By the way—we thought it might be best not to let on to Dan or anything."

"Naturally."

"You'll probably get at least as much as you got last year."

"I sure could use it."

"It won't come from me. I don't know anything about the whole thing."

"Of course. It comes from?"

"The Birds. Benny."

Benny Johnson was president of the Townbirds. He once played football at the U—rather badly, although he had since managed to convince everybody he was practically All-American—and now he was sort of a businessman-around-town, with a lot of money in a lot of places. Once he even ran for Congress—A PENNY FOR BENNY was his slogan —but God again showed his partiality to our nation, and Benny was defeated.

"Fine," I said. But Pug looked sort of sour. "Say, is this okay with you? I don't want it if it's not."

"It's okay," he said. "I wouldn't want Dan in any kind of trouble."

"You just don't like the idea that Benny suggested it—?"

"I suggested it."

I didn't say anything. One of the reasons I get along so well with people is that I know when not to say anything. What Pug didn't like was that he had to go to Benny and ask. He didn't like asking for things, and he didn't like Benny.

"I don't want you trying to play detective or nothing," he said after a minute. "Just be like a close friend—help him with his studies, see that everything is going along okay."

"Of course."

"That's all, then."

I got up. "Are you going over to school? Maybe you could drop me off at Dan's dorm. I might as well start right in."

"Don't you ever walk anywhere? All right. I'm going anyway."

Caroline was in the kitchen, putting away groceries. We hadn't heard her come in.

"Hello, Pug," she said. She was thirty, eight years younger than Pug. Kind of thin, with black hair and long legs and black eyes that were always moving uncertainly, she had reached that peak of young-wife beauty that good-looking girls hold for a few years before they begin looking like clubwomen.

"'Lo," Pug said. He didn't kiss her or anything. He hardly looked at her. "You know Jack here?"

"We've met," she said.

"Hello, Mrs. Walters," I said.

She kept on working. "Will you be home for supper, Pug?"

"I don't know," he said. "Let's go, Jack."

I said good-by to Caroline and we left.

CHAPTER THREE

After Pug drove off, I waited inside the vestibule of Dancer's dorm for a few minutes, then walked two blocks to the Kappa Delt House. I had to get the story in before I could spend any time with Dancer.

The deal on Dancer sounded good. I had gotten to like the kid last year—although we weren't exactly best friends —and at any rate figured it'd be easier working with one dolt than five, even if it meant a little running around keeping track of him. Dancer wouldn't be hard to control; he was something of a model American boy in his own way. And the money: Pug said at least as much as last year, and I had a feeling it'd be more. Benny might even keep paying through the whole school year. After all, Dancer could flunk out or get in trouble just as easily in February as in October.

Between Benny and the *Standard,* the money from the cigarettes, and whatever I could pick up writing term papers and taking exams, this looked like my best year so far. My family had no money at all—my father is what he likes to call a Parks Guard, in Crotona Park in the Bronx—and either I made it on my own or I didn't make it. When I couldn't get a football scholarship anywhere, I decided to come to the U on my own as an out-of-state student, be-

cause it was cheaper than the private colleges and the
idea of traveling West appealed to me. For getting the high-
est score on the placement exams, I got a two-hundred-
dollar scholarship. That's the biggest they have for academic
work. I would have got three thousand dollars for football, but if you can't afford the trolley, the kids in New
York used to say, you can always hook a ride on the back,
and we used to, clinging to the rear like flies. So I got a job
on the *Standard*, supposedly to cover all newsworthy campus activities, which meant football. Through covering the
team I got to know Pug, which led to his hiring me to tutor
some of his boys. We defined tutoring pretty broadly; I
probably wrote more themes and term papers last year than
any twenty other students. I felt I more or less deserved
an education, and since there wasn't anyone around interested in giving me one, I'd get it any way I could. It was
either that or becoming a butcher or a machinist or something.

When I got to the fraternity, it was full of pledges who
had come back early to cut the grass and clean up the
House, but there were only a few overlords around, and
I got to my room without bumping into any of them. One
of the rules our Founding Fathers had dreamed up was
that no two Kappa Delts should ever meet without a few
minutes of pleasant social conversation. A simple hello was
deemed inadequate to the Fraternity ideal.

I typed up the story, inked in a few changes, and headed
back downstairs. Once I have a story in my head, I can
get it on paper in no time. Unfortunately, I met Harry
Giffling, our Worthy Master Supreme. Giffling's great moment had come as a freshman; he spent a week drooling
over an unshaded dorm window a block away, watching
the girl inside dress and undress, before he bought himself
a pair of binoculars and discovered it was a boy's dorm.

I gave him thirty seconds of pleasant conversation before trying to break away, but he wanted to speak more; he touched my sleeve. Giffling was a great sleeve-toucher. He saw it as a very portentous and moving gesture.

"I gotta get down to the paper. Rush story."

"Just want to remind you—you're up for pledge supervision tomorrow. Weed clearance."

"Don't think I'll be able to make it, Harry. I'm working full time on the *Standard* until school starts."

"We realize you're busy, but you're still supposed to carry your share."

"I'll make it up later in the year."

"You always say that, but you never—"

"I'm really sorry, Giff, but I do have to run. Let me know next time my turn comes up, okay?"

I walked a block to Third Street, surveyed the cars at the curb, then reached through the open window of a '51 Ford and pulled the hood latch. I went around front, lifted the hood and stood alongside it in the street. The next car going by stopped.

"Trouble, son?"

"A little." I flashed my press card. "I have to get down to the *Standard* by deadline. Are you going by there?"

"Sure, hop in." He was sorta middle-aged, but not too prosperous. The car was a '54 Pontiac.

"What kinda trouble you have?"

"Number three cylinder."

"Blew?"

"Yeah."

He shook his head solemnly. "I had a Ford once—nothing but trouble."

"That's the way it goes," I said. People kid me about getting things for nothing, but one way or another you end up paying. For rides, you pay with talk. The funny thing about Dancer, who's so quiet all the time, is that he loves hitchhiking. He even hitchhikes to school and back all the time—he comes from Pennsylvania—because he says he enjoys it. If I had the dough, I'd cut my thumb off before I'd ever stick it in a driver's face again.

"What do you do on the *Standard?*"

"Political reporting. Governor's in town, you know."

"I didn't."

"Officially, he's inspecting the new law building."

The man nodded. "What's he really doing?"

"Giving Irvine the word on the team."

"Really?"

"Sure. Says the other governors rib hell out of him with the team we got."

"No wonder. I'm a U man myself, you know. Thirty-nine. We used to have *teams* in those days."

"Yes, sir," I said. "Those were the days."

He let me out in front of the *Standard* office.

"I don't guess none of that real dope will get in the paper, eh?"

"Not a chance. I shouldn't even have mentioned it."

"I'll keep it quiet."

"Thanks."

The *Standard* offices were in what had once been a mortuary, which struck the paper's critics as wonderfully appropriate. When the population started drifting to the suburbs, the mortuary followed, and the newspaper moved in. The paper wasn't too bad, I guess. It had a good circulation, because Midland was the county seat and also the biggest town between the two population centers in the northern and southern tips of the state. The *Standard's* politics, however, were rather hazy and mugwumpy. They often changed abruptly, depending upon which of the state's political leaders were momentarily more successful in reinforcing G. A. Magnus' view of himself as a political seer. G. A. Magnus was the editor and publisher. The

only issues on which the *Standard* never wavered were its
support of wildlife conservation (Magnus was a great
hunter) and federal aid to farmers (protecting the American
heritage of the soil), and its firm opposition to federal aid
to education (socialism). Magnus had gone to the University, but had not graduated—according to his version, it
was because he had to go and fight World War I, but the
rumor around campus was that he had flunked out. None-
theless, he was first and last a University man, and was now
a power on the Board of Regents, where he served to spur
the other regents into doing something realistic about the
football team. *Realistic* was one of his favorite words.

The sports department was downstairs, in what probably
used to be the embalming room. It wasn't really a department; there was Andy Rivers, who had a glass-enclosed
cubicle for an office; Don Ames, whose main distinction was
that he had once lasted six months on the Cincinnati
Enquirer before being fired; a kid named Alfred something
who was hot from our very own and absolutely worthless
school of journalism; and me. There were also four desks,
three Underwood typewriters (of which two worked), a
lot of pictures and schedules on the wall, and a hanging
newspaper file. People always talk about the look of a
typical newspaper office, with all the reporters with their
hats back on their heads and everything, but what always
got me was the smell. I think it was the paste.

Don Ames was sitting at a desk and leaning over a typewriter, chin in hand. Andy was in his glass cage.

"How's it going, Ace?" was Don's greeting, offered in
the witty, sardonic style for which newspapermen, especially embittered, hard-drinking ones, are famous.

"Okay," I said.

"World come to an end yet?"

"Not yet."

"Have to save it for the next edition, I guess."

He resumed staring at his Underwood, and I knocked on the glass door. Andy looked up and nodded.

"It's not exactly early," he said. Even when he wasn't talking very loud, his voice had a penetrating quality.

"I wrote it up and brought it right over," I said. I put the story on his desk. He didn't even look down at it.

"Maybe I'll be able to brush it up a bit, work some of it into my column."

"Sure," I said. I knew what that meant. He wiped his forehead. Sometimes I think it was just a nervous movement. He had probably been sitting in his chair contemplating his typewriter for the last hour, though, which accounted for his not being overly winded.

"Did you get any decent shots?"

"I think so. The old lady really gave us a hard time but—"

"Okay." He buzzed a button on his desk and the kid from stereo came in. "Gimme some prints on these." The kid took the plates and left. "I don't like your practice stories," Andy said. "They sound phony. What are you doing, rewriting last year's stories?"

"Of course not. I—"

"Where were you Tuesday?"

"At practice, sir. I go every day."

"I came by at three-thirty."

"I had just left."

"Kinda early, wasn't it?"

"I didn't leave practice. I went to the locker room just about then. Planters hurt his leg in the two-on-one drill and I wanted to see if he was all right."

"You didn't have nothing on it in the story."

"Because he was all right."

"Did you stay in the locker room then until five o'clock?"

"No. I watched practice from the runway. I wanted

to see Jensen about the drops—I heard they were dropping
four or five guys, and I wanted to get their—"

"All right, all right. I just want you there every day. I
don't want no more fairy stories."

"I'm always there," I said. "You don't have to worry
about it."

"I haven't forgotten that baseball game."

"That'll never happen again, Mr. Rivers."

"It better not."

Whenever he thought of that, he boiled. It still bothered
me a little too. Last spring the baseball team played
Iowa State, away, and for some reason Andy, who covers
all games—I just do the practices and the leg work—
couldn't go, and sent me. It was a night game, ending just
about deadline, so he told me to send in only a line score
if we lost. If we won, he'd hold up the paper for a full
box and a big story, because we'd have tied for the conference title. Well, by the fifth inning, we were behind
12–1, and the box score was really a mess, with Iowa State
scoring about every two minutes. So I figured the hell with
it and stopped keeping score. But college baseball is pretty
unpredictable; once they start kicking the ball around anything can happen. Things began happening in the eighth
and kept right on happening in the ninth. I sure was rooting
hard for Iowa State. Unfortunately, when it was over we
had won 15–13, so I faked the box and most of the story.
All I had right, I think, was the score. Andy gave it a big
page-one play and the next day the whole team descended
on him, led by the first baseman, who had gone four-for-
five. We had him one-for-six. I explained to Andy that the
Western Union operator had scrambled everything, but I
don't think he fully believed me.

He fired me, of course, and the kid who replaced me was
honest as hell, but dumb. I sent him down, although Andy
didn't know it. I told the kid not to mention my name since

Andy had just booted me out. After waiting a week, I dropped in casually on Andy, who jumped at the chance of rehiring me. He made me promise to be good and everything, which I did, but the kid was so bad I think he would have taken me back anyhow. In spite of what everyone says, most people prefer the brilliant-dishonest type over the opposite. They feel more at home because they think they're brilliant themselves, and they know they're dishonest.

"And gimme a feature tomorrow on Dancer," Andy said. He still hadn't looked at my story. "Get a little life in it this time, all right?"

"I just did one on him last week."

"I want another one. Get a different angle. Make it interesting. And bring it in early for a change."

"Yes, sir."

"The Birds are meeting at noon. Come over and work up something for the column."

"Yes, sir."

"We'll see you then. Unless I drop down to practice."

"I'll be there if you do. Good night, sir." I started out, then flipped a pack of Lords on his desk. "Here, sir. On me."

"I never smoke them," he said, making no effort to give them back. "They taste lousy."

"Pass them along to a friend," I said.

I lifted the hood of a '53 Dodge and got back to campus around eight o'clock. It was a nice, crisp fall evening— football weather, as people insisted on calling it. I always liked the paved walks on campus at night, curving around the trees, with the lamp posts lit and the evening smell of the grass in the air. Most of the dorms were dark, and everything was quiet, more like a park than a campus, but I felt depressed thinking about all the students coming.

There were twelve thousand in all, and the campus never looked beautiful after they arrived—a bunch of kids in raked red sports cars and a lot of stupid girls squeaking and giggling to each other. One time I walked past a couple of girls outside Humanities Hall, and one of them was saying, "Which comes first again now, Plato or Aristotle? I never can get them straight." There was something about the way she said it that really bothered me.

The only place lighted up was the athlete's wing of Holley Hall, known also as Ape Hall, or sometimes The Jungle. Guys who had free rides lived there. Most of them were football, with a few baseball and basketball players and an occasional swimmer or track man. Football got the real money, though, and the football players knew it. Breakage and damage in their rooms ran about ten times the average around campus. Students had to pay for things they broke, and football players didn't; it was part of the free ride. There wasn't much a football player couldn't get away with. A few years back three of them were caught breaking into the math office to steal copies of a final. This happens all the time around schools, not just with football players, and everybody more or less accepts it, the way they accept phony themes and cheating on exams. But when a plain student gets caught stealing exams, for instance, he gets expelled. The football players were suspended for the rest of the semester—about two weeks—and then allowed to return. Quietly. The whole thing was handled quietly. But what the hell, I don't see anything so terrible about it. That's the way things are, and not only around colleges. Everyone knows what the judge is going to say when the banker's son in his new Caddy crashes into a '43 Plymouth driven by some spic from the back side of town. It's just that around campuses football players are the bankers' sons, and plain students the spics.

Dancer had a single room on the second floor of Ape

Hall, but he wasn't there. I checked down the hall with
some of the other boys from the squad, who were making
a big racket wrestling with each other and horsing around.
Football players are always horsing around. I guess that's
how they manage to break so much.

"Hey—seen Dancer?"

"He jumped out the window before—we been waiting
to hear him splat."

They all considered themselves great jokers. "I gotta see
him," I said. "Where is he?"

"We ain't seen him."

"None of you seen him?"

"No."

After trying Dancer's room again, I went downstairs.
Last year he hardly went out at all and so didn't have any
hangouts that I knew of. But I had no intention of running
around looking for him anyhow; I did my duty by dropping over.

I called Peggy from the dorm phone and told her I was
coming over. I had half forgotten about her with the rush
of things. "Your father still waiting?"

"He hasn't been doing anything *but* waiting. Mother too.
But Daddy told her to go upstairs when you come. He's
really all worked up."

"Hey, he doesn't think you're pregnant, does he?"

"Of course not. Mother knows I'm not. I'm sure he's asked
her."

"Okay. You go upstairs too when I come."

"I thought we'd speak to him together and—"

"It'll be better this way, man to man and everything."

"Well, I hope so . . . Jack—you do love me, don't you?"

"Would I be coming over like this to see your father and
everything if I didn't?"

"But you never *say* you love me any more."

"I've been giving all my attention to this thing with your father. I think about it all the time."

"Well . . . all right. After tonight everything will be better, won't it?"

"Much," I said.

On the way out I met the boys from the room upstairs and asked them where they were going.

"Smoky's."

"You can give me a lift then."

We all piled into Chuck Janowski's car and drove off.

"You going to Smoky's too?" Chuck asked. He was a tackle.

"No. Walnut and Sixteenth."

"Hey—that's about two miles *past* Smoky's!"

"It's on a direct line. It'll only take a minute."

"Christ," he said, but he drove me out anyhow. He had a raked and souped-up '59 Studebaker with dual exhausts, and it sounded like a jet. He drove at his normal city speed, about fifty.

He let me off in front of Peggy's house, under the big elm. "Thanks for the ride, Chuck."

He drove off without saying anything and I walked up the path to the porch and knocked on the door. Peggy came outside, closing the door behind her. She kissed me and hung on.

"Promise you'll be nice to him, Jack. I do so want it to work out all right."

"It'll work out fine. You just introduce me and run upstairs."

"Here, let me wipe the lipstick off first."

CHAPTER FOUR

Peggy took me into the living room, where her father was standing near the fireplace, staring across at us as we entered. He was a big man, with a lot of fat under his eyes and great round glasses through which he squinted as if in pain. He worked in some office in town, but wasn't anything. Peggy always mumbled something about him being "in business" and then dropped the subject. He wore a dingy gray suit with a vest. The room had a lot of lamp shades with plastic covers over them.

He stood there glowering, waiting for Peggy to introduce me, but she was having trouble finding her voice. She was all dressed up, and I remembered very fondly the tight black dress she had on. She had bleached white-blonde hair and looked very good in the dress, but it was mainly the buttons I remembered. It's funny—a few buttons really mean a lot to a girl. Maybe it all started with Adam and Eve, or some long-tailed monkey, according to which school you belong to, but by the time the girls get to college it all pretty much boils down to a couple of buttons, all their inborn caution and indecision, all the old wives' tales they've ever heard, all eighteen years of parental guidance and pious Sunday school finger-wagging, all the dire warnings from mothers and maiden aunts and older, previously unbuttoned sisters—and after all this, everything depends on which guy they let do what with a few chips from the bone of the ass of some wild animal.

"This is Jack," Peggy announced finally. She was so nervous she was fingering the buttons. "You . . . You've heard me speak of him."

"How do you do," he said from the fireplace. His voice was kind of stiff and weighted down.

"Pleased to meet you," I said. We waited, and then I looked toward Peggy.

"I think I'll go upstairs and join mother now."

"Very well," he said.

She left, walking in her heels and in the tight dress with short steps, her legs from the knees down perpendicular to the floor, as if she were bucking a strong current. I waited for the old man to offer me a chair, which he did when he saw me looking at one. He did it without saying anything, by moving his hand a little, as if he were shaking a fly off his wrist.

"Very nice house you have here."

"We like it."

I waited. "Was there anything in particular you wanted to speak to me about, sir?"

"There was."

I waited a bit more, then took out a pack of Lords and got up to offer him a cigarette—I didn't think it'd look good to him a whole pack—but he shook his head.

"None of our family smoke."

"Of course." I sat down again. Peggy smoked all the time.

"Peggy's mother has passed along some . . . disquieting information about my daughter," he said. He was still standing up. You could see he had the whole thing memorized; when he paused it wasn't to think of the word, but to remember it. "Which, I might add, my daughter had the honesty not to deny."

"What kind of information, sir?"

"We'll come to that in a moment. How old are you?"

"Twenty-one."

"Peggy said you were twenty-three."

"She must have got it wrong. I don't think I told her that."

"You what?"

"I don't think I told her I was twenty-three, sir. I think I told her I was twenty-one."

He glared at me and shuffled his feet a bit.

"Peggy also said you were a junior."

"Not exactly, sir . . . not technically."

"What do you mean?"

"Well, I'm sort of a sophomore. I mean, normally I would *be* a sophomore, but I had some trouble with a couple of courses and—"

"Peggy said you were a good student."

"Well . . . that was certainly very nice of her, sir."

"What year *are* you in?"

"Actually, I'm a sophomore . . . but of course I won't officially become one until I make up a couple of courses and—"

"You mean you're still a freshman?"

"Only on paper, sir."

"All right. All right. What are you studying?"

"A little bit of everything, sir. Sort of a well-rounded program. Well-balanced. Sure you won't have a cigarette, sir?"

"I do *not* smoke. How do you expect to earn a living when you graduate?"

"I don't, sir—at least, not right away. I've been thinking of going on for a Ph.D. in philology."

His mouth was working a bit now.

"That's more or less like semantics," I said. "Language."

"Of course," he said. "But what are you going to do with it?"

"That's so far off, sir, that I don't really think about it too much."

"How far off?"

"Oh, I don't know . . . eight, ten years, I guess. Ph.D.s take a long time. Although you certainly do learn a lot along the—"

"How do you expect to live meanwhile? Even Ph.D.s have to eat."

"There are some very generous fellowships available, sir, and I hope—if my grades pick up a bit—to win one. Some pay as high as fourteen or fifteen hundred dollars a year."

He winced and was quiet again for a while. "Have you been *using* Peggy?"

"I think very highly of your daughter, sir."

"You haven't answered my question."

"As a general rule, sir, I don't like to discuss such personal questions, even with a girl's family. I feel—"

"A general rule! How many times have you—" He cut himself short. He had probably been telling himself all day not to lose his temper. He calmed down a bit and spoke very evenly: "Have you given any thought to marriage?"

"Oh, yes," I said. "Frequently."

"I mean in reference to my daughter."

"Oh. Well, we *have* discussed it, sir. But there is, of course, the religious problem."

"What religious problem?"

"You see, sir, I'm Jewish. Very Orthodox. My parents brought me up to—"

"Peggy never said anything about that."

"I'm not sure that I told her."

"You mean you lied to her?"

"No, sir. I just never told her, I think."

He was breathing like a horse by this time and finally sat down. "You don't look Jewish," he said, examining my face.

I didn't say anything. I almost told him the joke about the Chinese Jew, but decided against it.

"I know what's been going on between you two," he said abruptly.

I continued my silence.

"When I asked you to come, I told my wife, and I told Peggy, there could be only two choices: either you would ask to marry her, or I would tell you not to see her again."

"Yes, sir."

"She'll get over her dishonor, she might even learn something from it . . . and I would rather have her ten times dishonored than let her ruin her life marrying someone who would not even tell her the truth." He paused, rather satisfied with the speech, I think, and then blinked. "For all I know, you may not even be telling me the truth."

"Yes, sir."

"*Have* you been telling me the truth?"

"I always try to tell the truth, sir."

"Please go. I don't want any more of this."

"Would you prefer that I not say good-by to Peggy?"

"I would prefer that you not see her again. Ever."

"We were in the same class this summer—but we could probably avoid that in the future."

"I think you have a great deal to learn from life. I don't think you have very commendable attitudes."

I got up. "I'm afraid you're right, sir, but I want you to know I'll try to improve. I think what you've said tonight will really help."

"I hope so. Please go."

"Good night, sir. You've certainly been very understanding."

He didn't say anything else, so I just left, going out the

front door and down the porch, past the swing, down the
front path. It was pretty late and the night was chilly, but
the grass and the trees smelled just fine. Peggy had been
nice enough, especially for the summer, when most of the
other girls were away and the campus was overrun with
middle-aged fifth-grade teachers taking courses in Adjustment Psychology of the Child from Five to Ten, but now
the others would be coming back and I didn't feel too bad
about being loose again. At least relatively loose—my contacts weren't limited to coeds, and I had one non-dating
friend whom I saw occasionally with great pleasure. I'm
not really good-looking, but I've always managed to do all
right, and part of the freedom I felt walking down that
path came from my confidence that I wouldn't have much
trouble finding Peggy's successor. Because even though I
wasn't handsome, I wasn't ugly either. Actually, I looked
like a football player—like a not-very-good guard—which
is kind of funny, because someone like Dancer, for instance,
when you see him in clothes, doesn't look at all like a football player. But I do. I'm rather thick and broad, almost
fat. When I was in shape in high school I weighed 184,
but after that I never managed to get much under 200.
And my face doesn't make me appear too bright. I *look*
more or less like you'd expect a not-very-good guard to *be*.

I make up for these disadvantages, however, by avoiding
good-looking girls. There's too much competition for the
queens, which leads them to put an unrealistically high
value on what they have to offer. Too much money and
effort has to be spent that probably won't get you anywhere anyhow. For one thing, those girls know all the patterns and sometimes like to play along for kicks until the
time of inevitable decision comes, when they just smile
prettily and pull out. They don't always pull out, of course,
but they get so many offers that they have to pull out on
some of them. I've always done well by sticking to the

plain ones, the shy ones, the scholarly-looking ones, the ones with unstylish hairdos or poor taste in clothes, the bad dancers, the lousy conversationalists. I avoid, of course, the fat, the ugly, the stupid. What I look for are signs of uneasiness, of prior unsuccess, and once in a while I even get a real beauty, like Marie Wu, who happened to be Chinese. Anyhow, I take on these imperfect but not unattractive girls one at a time, concentrating my efforts. Most of them are defenseless; they've never had the chance of working up through the minor leagues like the queens, who've been fighting off guys since Brownie days. Tempering my firmness with patience and understanding, I gradually break through the virgin ice, restore their confidence in themselves, and heat them up a bit, always to find that the kind of well-directed arrows of passion that serve only to chill their beautiful (and knowledgeable) sisters turn these untutored plain Janes into roaring, willing volcanoes.

I never, of course, fall in love. Love involves too much of a person; it cuts into his time, freedom, money, rationality, integrity. No matter how truly in love you are, somewhere along the line you have to start lying, faking, saying things you don't believe. And if I really loved someone, I'd probably feel bad about doing that. Just the way I can write themes and even take exams for people, or make up stories for the *Standard* and phony reports for Royal Kings without any qualms, because all I'm doing is upholding my end of what's a pretty shady deal all around. But if Andy Rivers and Benny and the University and everything—everything—were on the level, I'd probably feel bad about these things too.

Besides, love takes the joy out of romance. I could have just dropped Peggy, for instance; and if I had been in love with her and had lost interest, that's what I would have done—angrily, bitterly. But this way I got a pleasant evening with her father out of it.

Anyhow, I walked down that nice little path toward the elm tree feeling good about everything, smelling the grass and the trees, and thinking of that still unknown girl with chubby legs or thick glasses who was at that very moment probably off in Topeka or Sault Ste. Marie or Evansville shyly packing her little suitcase and dreaming of the adventures awaiting her at the big university, when something popped up behind the hedge.

"*Peggy!*"

"Ssssshhh . . ." She grabbed my arm and hurried me along the sidewalk, away from the house. She pulled me behind the big tree in front of the next house.

"What are you doing out here?"

"I sneaked out before. I've been waiting for you. I was afraid Daddy would send you off and—"

"He did send me off. We're not supposed to see each other again. Ever."

She grabbed me around the neck. "Oh, Jack—we can't let him do that. We'll meet in secret. He doesn't have to know."

"He *is* your father . . ."

"I don't care. He's an old fuddy. I'll leave home. I'll live in a dorm or a rooming house or something."

"But, Peggy . . . I wouldn't feel right running around behind his back. It wouldn't be honest."

"Don't say that, Jack. We can't let him ruin everything for us." She was still hanging on, moving around and everything. I was attracted to Peggy in the first place because although she was shy and not really beautiful and not quite as intelligent as I'd like, she had a terrific figure, very full, very pronounced, and all that hanging on and squirming under a tree on a dark street was hard to take. I began to reconsider. After all, the new girls wouldn't be in for a couple of days, and it would take at least a week to line up someone. And when the time came, I could count on an

ally in Peggy's old man. Meanwhile, I had to admit that
I did sort of like Peggy. Besides, I needed a ride back to
the campus.

"Do you have your car?" I whispered.

She nodded furiously and we ran to the corner, where
she had wisely parked. The old man couldn't afford to
give her much of a car, but it was a sturdy '51 Ford and we
had gotten good use from it that summer.

"We shouldn't stay out too late," I said as we drove off,
with Peggy driving. I never learned how to drive. "Your
father will be sore anyhow and—"

"Where should we go?"

"The reservoir."

She drove a few miles out of town and turned onto a side
road. We drove past the big clearing that overlooked the
reservoir—it was too well known to other students and to
the cops—and cut into another dirt road that practically no
one knew. It led to a grassy hill on the other side of the
water. The view wasn't too romantic or anything, but we
always had the place to ourselves. We parked and I was all
set to get the blanket from the trunk when Peggy took my
arm.

"Jack . . ."

"Yes?"

"Maybe we shouldn't do this any more . . . I mean, if
you feel so bad about Daddy and everything. I don't want
you feeling guilty."

"I'll get over it," I assured her. Already, I was glad I
hadn't gone ahead and dropped her. She was really a hell
of a good girl. A lot of fun. Unpretentious. She didn't
lecture me on my attitude toward life or anything, the way
a lot of people do. She was too pure of heart for that
and, in her own way, remarkably innocent. I moved closer
along the seat and put her head on my shoulder. I ran

my hand through her hair; she had gone all out when she bleached it, and it had a silver glow in the dark.

"I wouldn't want anything to spoil it for us," she said. "I'd rather not do it at all than have it spoiled."

"Of course. So would I." I started, gradually. She didn't stop me or anything. I did it very delicately. "But nothing will be spoiled," I assured her. "It'll be better than ever."

"I just want it the way it's always been. I want it to be perfect, always, forever."

"Me too," I said. I kissed her ear and bit her a little. "Let's get out," I whispered.

She nodded and snuggled tight once more and then sat up. "Oh! . . . my dress is all open!"

"Yes," I said. "Isn't that lovely?"

It was after midnight when we drove back over the dirt road and onto the side road and finally out to the highway.

"It's awfully sweet of you to drive me home all the time," I said.

"I enjoy doing it."

"I just wanted you to know I appreciated it."

She laughed and patted my knee. She was really a sweet girl. I was feeling good and she was feeling good. Things had worked out well at the reservoir. They always did for us. For a shy and relatively inexperienced girl, Peggy possessed a remarkable ability to relax and enjoy herself.

We drove along Baxter Boulevard, the big street connecting the University with the residential section of town. Pizzerias and bars and ice cream parlors and used-car lots lined the street, most of them dark now. Smoky's, though, was still open and in fact seemed pretty busy, with quite a few cars in the lot. Smoky's was the big hangout for University students and soldiers from McNair Army Base, mainly because Smoky's served beer to almost anyone.

Once in a while they'd get fined when some kid's mother or some church complained, but arrangements had been made with the Midland police force, and Smoky's was never seriously bothered.

As we were driving past, I noticed a crowd of guys standing around outside, and they didn't look right. I had a terrible feeling that something was wrong, and that somehow it was wrong for me. I get feelings like that occasionally, and they're very dependable.

"Pull over. Quick."

"What?"

"By Smoky's. You've gone past it—turn around and pull over. I gotta see someone there."

"I'll go with you."

"No, you go on home. Your father will be raging."

And then I heard the siren, still pretty far away. Peggy swung around and stopped at the curb. I jumped out.

"Go on, now. Go home. I'll see you tomorrow."

I ran across the loose gravel of the parking lot. About twenty guys, all of them excited and noisy, stood in a rough circle not far from the entrance. A window had been smashed and there was a good deal of broken glass on the ground. In the center of the crowd two guys had squared off. One was a soldier, stiffly poised, his nose bloody, a black switchblade in his hand. The other was Dancer.

CHAPTER FIVE

The siren had got considerably louder by the time I reached the crowd. The soldier was young but pretty big. Dancer, thank God, was unmarked. He hadn't even worked up a sweat; he looked very cool in his slacks and sport shirt, like some casual junior executive on his day off, except that he had his fists up, in a beautiful classic prize fighter's stance that he had probably been born with, the way he had been born with that perfect halfback's gait of his.

I did not, however, spend much time admiring his form. I did not even spend much time mulling over the implications of the fact that on this, my first night as his protector, as his goddamn guardian angel, he had managed to get himself engaged in a knife fight at Smoky's at one-thirty in the morning—although these things did run through my mind in a hurried and haphazard way.

"MPs coming! Cops!" I shouted, charging straight into the crowd. The siren was right near by. "Let's get out of here!"

The crowd had been pretty intent on Dancer and the soldier, who were eying each other sullenly, but I stirred everybody up enough to get them all looking around in different directions. I charged head-on into the middle of

the circle before anyone was ready for me and grabbed
the soldier from behind and wrapped my left leg around
his legs and shoved him toward three of his buddies. He
lurched into their arms and they caught him and held on.

"Quick," I yelled. "The MPs'll get him. They're on their
way."

The siren sounded right on top of us now and the crowd
broke noisily and began to scatter. I didn't watch what
happened to the soldier. I just wanted him out of the way,
because I knew Dancer wouldn't come with me if the other
guy was still standing there ready to fight. Dancer wasn't
much for fighting, but whatever had got him angry enough
to fight in the first place would probably keep him angry for
some time. Besides, this way Dancer had a chance to
recognize me; even though I was bigger, and probably as
strong, he was awful quick and I was afraid he might lay
me out before he realized who I was. I grabbed his arms
and started dragging him away.

"C'mon, Dan—*Move!*"

He shook me off. Luckily, Chuck Janowski was still
around, and I was never happier to see a 230-pound tackle
in my life.

"Chuck! We gotta get Dan out of here!"

Together we managed to get Dancer moving, across the
lot and around the building to the rear parking area.
Dancer saw that everyone was leaving, including the soldier
with the knife. We got into Chuck's car just as the siren
hit a last rising burst right out front.

"The back way," I told Chuck. "Over the curb."

He bumped down easily and drove slowly for a few
blocks so the duals wouldn't blast, and then hit the pedal
and circled back to Baxter Boulevard, about five blocks
from Smoky's.

"I kinda hate leaving the other guys there," he said.

"You can go back after you drop us off."

He was really moving along. I don't think he felt safe under forty-five.

Dancer was sitting on the outside, on my right, looking out the window. I could tell he was really worked up.

"What the hell you getting in fights for?" I said. I was sore now that it was all over.

He shrugged. "I shouldna let you drag me away. I shoulda got that guy."

"The cops would have thrown you in jail—disturbing the peace and everything. What are you trying to do, ruin yourself?"

Dancer looked out the window and didn't say anything.

"How'd it start?" Chuck asked. "I didn't see nothing happen or nothing."

"It don't matter," Dancer said.

"You got in one good punch," Chuck said. "Almost put him through the window."

"I wanted to get him," Dancer said.

I had never seen him so angry before. He's really a very mild kid—shy, almost. Red Warwick, the freshmen coach, even used to give him talks about aggressiveness and the killer instinct.

Chuck left us at Ape Hall, then roared off for his friends. Dancer started up to his room—without even saying thanks for getting me out of there, or come on up, or good night, but I went up anyhow. He lay on his bed with his clothes still on and I sat in the basket chair looking at him. His room wasn't as messy as mine, with books and papers and cigarette cartons around, but looked instead as if someone had come in and decided to take a shower and so left a few clothes about, shirt, socks, trousers, but would be back in a minute to get dressed and move on again.

Dan lay staring at the ceiling with his hands cupped behind his head. He was still worked up.

"You feeling all right?"

"Yeah."

No one said anything for a while after that. If you hung around with Dancer much you got used to long quiet stretches. You could be in a room with him for an hour—and not doing anything, just sitting there—without getting a word.

"You could've got hurt, you know. The guy could've cut you all up."

He just lay there looking up at the ceiling. It didn't bother me. I was used to him, and if I had to play nurse-maid to one of our apes, I could have done a lot worse. If he'd stay out of knife fights, that is.

"How'd the fight start?"

"It don't matter. Forget it."

"All right. I'll wait."

You had to push with Dancer. He didn't mind—he just ignored it, really—and he was so quiet and easy that you couldn't get anything out of him if you didn't push. But in spite of his shortcomings, I liked him, which proves I'm incapable of envy, because if there's one guy in the world I should hate it's Dancer. Ever since I was a kid I wanted to be an athlete, any kind of an athlete. I finally concentrated on football because I was big enough for it and best at it. And I really concentrated. I didn't miss a practice throughout four years of high school. Over the summers I did the special exercises the coach recommended to all the kids but that none of the kids, except me, did. I played four-wall handball to keep up my wind. I did leg-twists to build up my ankles and harden my calves. I did deep-knee bends—thousands of them—to thicken my thighs. I practiced my stance, memorized plays, knew every assignment perfectly. I made my kid brother stand over me while

I crouched down and had him hold my head in his hands and lean on me while I tried to twist free, because this was good for the neck and back muscles. I read books on football and probably knew as much about it as the coach did. I talked football all the time, all winter, all summer, all the time. And what happened? I made third string as a sophomore, second string as a junior, and, in the culminating glory of my senior year, alternated at first string with another guy. I say we alternated, but actually he played twice as much as I did. It killed me that someone with a mind like mine, and with my size, and with the knowledge I had and the practice time I spent, should be such a bumbler once I stepped on the field—but boy, I was a master bumbler.

For one thing, I had no reaction time. When the other guy charged left and I had been expecting him straight, I always moved a split-second too late and he'd be past me, or else would dump me while I was still off balance. Even worse, I had no instinct. I'd be positive the quarterback had only faked a handoff and would smash through marvelously to smother him. Then, getting up, thinking the cheers were for me, I'd see the halfback gliding away forty yards downfield. Sure, I made first team, more or less, as a senior—but this was DeWitt Clinton High School! I don't think three guys from DeWitt Clinton High School ever even got uniforms at a college, any college. Once I played against a guard from Stuyvesant who later played for Missouri. Now, Missouri wasn't the greatest team in the world, and this guy was no All-American, but he sure mauled me. I can still feel his cleats on my back.

What got me about Dancer was not that he was so good, but that a guy who could be so good on the field could be such an absolute boob off, and that he could have been that good on without really caring or trying. Even in high school he went out for the team only because in Humbolt,

Pennsylvania, the football coach was also the gym teacher; he saw Dancer playing catch in the school yard one day and shanghaied him onto the team. And then Dancer began to like the game a little, which should have been easy, because he was great from the minute he walked on the field. He even had fun playing; nobody took the game too seriously or spent too much time at it. Sure, the coach and the kids in school and all the Humboltians wanted to win, but that was all—they wanted to win and felt bad when they lost. And with Dancer, who was All-State three years in a row, they almost always won, because he could run circles around any of those high school tacklers, even in Pennsylvania, where tacklers with unpronounceable names come up out of the mines as frequently and as big as coal scuttles. That's how he got his nickname, which was natural enough for someone named Dan Danciewitz. He used to like to take a kickoff or a punt, and instead of trying to run up the field, just stay where he was and duck tacklers. He'd just wait there for them to come in at him and then step from side to side, feinting, ducking, dodging, dancing really, until four or five of them had gone flying past, and then he'd start moving up. This really drove the home folks wild in Humbolt, Pennsylvania, but Dancer didn't do it to show off or anything; he just thought it was fun, which I'm sure it must have been. Of course, when he tried it in his first intrasquad scrimmage with the freshman team at the University—and got away with it too, made the tacklers look like stumblebums—Red Warwick gave him the word. He told him this was college, and we don't play games here.

Dancer had not even wanted to play football in college. He had stopped enjoying it during his senior year at Humbolt, and kept on only because he had been convinced—by Red Warwick, who did most of our recruiting—that he'd be wasting a great educational opportunity by not going to college, and that football alone could give him this oppor-

tunity. "*They* don't give a damn about you," Warwick told
him, as he told all the boys he roamed the country to get,
meaning the administration, the school, "but *we* do, we're
giving you a chance to come where they wouldn't even give
you the right time; and don't worry, we'll take care of you,
we want you." But the fuss bothered Dancer: Andy's columns, the features (which he stopped reading after the
first week), the kids on campus staring at him, pointing
at him, Andy interviewing him like some visiting dignitary,
Benny slobbering over him, alumni stopping him on the
street to shake his hand and introduce themselves, to tell
him how glad they were to have him—as if he were a com-
modity, a thing, a new car fresh from the showroom that
they had just bought—and how eagerly they were awaiting
the day when he'd put the U on the football map once
more. Dan had simply assumed that Red Warwick was offering him the same deal he offered everyone else; it was
only after he got here that he realized he was the most ex-
pensively purchased guy on the squad.

But I think the main reason he came to us had little to
do with money. Everyone offered him money. He came to
us because Red Warwick sold him the biggest bill of goods
about his educational opportunities.

"He told me I could become an accountant, or maybe
even a teacher or an engineer or something like that,"
Dancer had told me last year.

"Red said that?"

"Yeah. Sure."

"He said you could be an engineer?"

"That's right."

"What about theoretical physics? Did you ever consider
theoretical physics—you know, like Einstein?"

"No, I never considered that."

"It's a coming field. I'm surprised Red didn't suggest it."

But Dancer wasn't the typical dumb football player who

fell into college like he was falling into a feather bed, who looked upon it as a nice place to lie around for four years and be well fed as long as he made it to the stadium for eight or nine Saturdays a year, and who wondered what the hell all those skinny kids with glasses were going to the library for all the time. (Where was it—this really happened at Arkansas or someplace—that one of the guys simply headed back to the farm after football season because he didn't realize he had to stay around the rest of the year?) But Dancer really *did* come to the University for an education. Really. He wanted to learn. He was bored to death by football, but he talked about the great opportunities it gave him like he was talking about the Holy Grail. His father worked in a coalpit or something, and Dancer was as serious about his studies as I used to be about football, and with equal success.

I never in my life saw anyone light up the way Dancer did the year before when once by accident he remembered something right from his history course and I said offhandedly that he really seemed to be catching on now. You'd think I'd just given him the Heisman Trophy. And then when Red Warwick told me that Dan seemed discouraged about his studies and that I should encourage him more and not get him worried, I went out of my way—really out of my way—to find things to praise him for, and boy, he sure ate it up. But you could tell him he was the greatest football player in the country—and really mean it—and he wouldn't even be listening. You hear of those athletes who don't read the stories about themselves in the papers and everything, which is usually a lot of bull, but Dancer was one guy who really didn't. And it wasn't one of these deals where he made a big point about not reading them; he just wasn't interested. They were paying him to play left halfback, and he did his job with about as much enthusiasm as he would if they were paying him to carry out bundles in a supermarket, although maybe he would have preferred the supermarket. At least it wouldn't scare him. As soon as football stopped being fun, it began to scare Dancer, not on the field but off, when he got to thinking about it. That was why he had a single room. Nights before a game he'd have a pretty bad time of it and didn't want anyone around. And it wasn't nervousness. Dancer isn't at all nervous, just scared. He'd have nightmares all the time and see himself carried off the field dead or mangled.

Dancer was still lying on the bed with his hands behind his head, still staring at the ceiling, and I probably could have stayed there all night waiting if I didn't push him. But then the phone rang in the hall downstairs.

Dancer swung his legs around and started for the door. "It's for me."

He hurried along the hall and down the stairs. You can hear a lot in a dorm at two o'clock in the morning and when I opened the door and leaned into the hall I could hear Dan talking, but couldn't make out his words. I decided against going down the hall to listen at the stairwell, because if he came up fast he might hear me running back. I closed the door and waited in the basket chair.

When he returned, Dan didn't say anything, but just started getting undressed.

"Was it really for you?"

"Yeah." He put on his pajama top. He wore heavy woolen pajamas all year, even in summer, and when it got chilly he added a couple of sweaters.

"Have anything to do with the fight?"

"Kinda."

"I'd hate to see you get in trouble. You oughta be more careful."

"You don't have to worry none about me."

"But I do. You're practically the best friend I have."

He shrugged.

"What happened?—you still haven't told me."

He sat on his bed in his woolen pajamas and thought for a moment. I was about the only guy Dancer ever talked to. He liked me, I think. He was impressed with my intelligence and everything.

"Nothing happened," he said finally. He had a habit of shrugging when he said anything beyond hello or good-by, as if telling you, as he was saying it, that what he was saying wasn't really important and you probably weren't interested anyhow. "The guy got wise, that's all."

"With you?"

"No."

"And the person he got wise with happens to be the person who called you up?"

"Yeah."

"Who happens to be female?"

"Yeah."

"Christ, Dan—what are you getting mixed up with girls for? I thought you learned better last year?"

He shrugged and said nothing. Dan spent most of last year running away from sorority girls. It got so after a while that he hardly left the dorm. Most of the girls were pretty good-looking, because the plain Janes I thrived on—and had to work like hell to get—wouldn't even try for Dancer. But Dancer just ran, sometimes literally. He was a little self-conscious, I think, about his lack of intelligence, and he was sure the girls just wanted to laugh at him. One time he did go out on a date that someone fixed up for him, and I don't know what the cute little Alpha Pi tried, but she sure scared the hell out of him.

"Who is it?" I asked. "Do I know her?"

"No. Her name's May Steiner."

"Very pretty name. What's she calling you up at two o'clock in the morning for? You're in training, you should be asleep now, not waiting for calls from girl friends."

"She wanted to find out if I was all right. I took her home first when the guy got wise."

"Why couldn't you call her?"

"Too late. She lives at the Y."

"The Y? Doesn't she go here?"

"She doesn't go anywhere. She works."

"Where?"

"In Broder's Department store. She sells stuff behind a counter." He shrugged. "I don't guess she's your type exactly, but she's very nice."

"You're gonna get yourself all tangled up and then—"

"I don't wanna talk about it, all right? You asked me and I told you."

"You've got a great opportunity here, Dan—education and everything—you could really make something out of yourself. I'd hate to see you throw—"

"I don't wanna talk about it. I gotta get to bed. We got practice at nine."

"Did she run after you?"

"No. She was just behind the counter. We started talking."

"You started talking to a girl—just like that?"

"Yeah."

"What'd you talk about?"

"Things."

"School hasn't started yet, you know. You're gonna have a lot of studying to do. You're not gonna have time to go running around with girls and hanging out at Smoky's and fighting off soldiers."

"She's gonna help me."

"Help you?"

"Yeah. With my studies and everything. She's really smart. Not like you, I mean—but smart."

"Well, if you're not gonna need me any more . . ."

"No . . . you helped me a lot. I don't mean this against

you or anything. I just mean we ain't gonna just be running around and everything. She's very serious."

"She sounds like a lovely girl."

"She is. She's very nice. I don't know if you'll like her or not, but she's very nice."

"Why don't you think I'll like her?"

"I don't know. Look, I gotta get to bed."

"When can I meet her?"

"Whenever you want, I guess."

"I'll take you up on that. By the way, did Pug tell you about our new system this year?"

"No."

"I'm gonna be too busy to tutor a whole bunch of guys again. I'm just gonna have one guy. You."

"Oh."

"I thought you'd like the idea. We'll be able to get a lot more done."

He spoke slowly. He was wrestling with thought, and it was painful. "I don't think you should do so much this year. That's what May says too. I should be doing more myself."

"Am I gonna hear all the time now what May says?"

"She's right. If I'm gonna go to college, I oughta do my own work more."

"You do your own work. I just help you. If you don't want my help any more, we can just forget the whole thing and let May run the show."

"I like your help and everything. It's just that I oughta write my own themes and stuff."

"You wrote your own themes last year."

"You always changed them."

"I offered constructive criticism."

"That's what I want this year—like you say, constructive criticism."

"All right. That sounds fine."

"I oughta go to sleep. Don't be sore. I really appreciate all your help."

"I'm not sore," I said. "Good night."

"I hope you like May when you meet her."

"I'm sure I will," I said.

CHAPTER SIX

My alarm went off, as usual, at six-thirty the next morning. Of course, it's pleasant and everything to sleep eight hours a night, but I learned early to get by on four. This was part of learning that if Jack Wyant wanted anything out of life, he'd have to scramble to get it. Even twenty-hour days always seemed crowded.

Like Dancer, I had a single room, but for different reasons: my long hours bothered other people, and I worked better alone. Generally, I got along okay at the House, as long as they left me alone. I joined because they had the best cook on campus and because I didn't like the idea of being stuck off in a dorm somewhere with a bunch of dead beats who couldn't even make a fraternity.

After a trip down the hall to wash and shave, I came back to get dressed. First, I put on the underwear my mother had dug into the piggy bank to buy me when I left for college. My mother was a great believer in well-made underwear. Then I dusted lightly under my arms with the can of powder I picked up at the gym, and put on one of the sports shirts I got for mentioning Koppel's Men's Store as a local landmark in a feature I did on fresh-man students finding their way around town. Next came the trousers that I got the same way, only from Mr. Klein of the School Sports Shop. The brown ripple soles were free a couple of summers back when I worked in a shoe store in New York; they had been returned by a customer after a few days' wear, and since they couldn't be resold, anyone who worked there could have them if they fit. They fit. Finally, I straightened my hair with the brush and comb Higgins let me have—the plastic display case was cracked —for a few extra packs of Royal Kings the last time we traded off.

Thus outfitted and prepared, I descended the stairs to begin my daily twenty-hour encounter with the forces of the World. As on all other days, these forces would, I had every reason to be certain, take as their motto the cry, JACK SHALL NOT PASS! And so, as on other days, I steeled myself as I proceeded down the steps with an equally stirring rally, to wit: HE DAMN WELL WILL!

There was, however, no immediate clash. The House was quiet, and not a single minion of the foe was yet up and stirring. I got my paper from the lawn, which the pledges had trimmed neatly, left the House paper where it was, and went into the kitchen to put up a pot of coffee. I found some stale rolls and looked at the paper while I ate alone in the big dining room whose walls were adorned with the handworked paddles that the faithful pledges had given their beloved older brothers.

The picture (sans mother) of Dancer autographing the football for the kid appeared as a four-column cut on the top of the sports page and, as he had promised, Andy managed to make use of my story in his column. I guess he never got around to brushing it up, though, because it appeared exactly as written:

A LOOK AT SPORTS

by

Andy Rivers

SPORTS EDITOR

MIDLAND STANDARD

PUG, DANCER VISIT
INJURED YOUNGSTER

Boy Thrilled As
Heroes Prove
Good Medicine

Young Timmy Rending sat up quietly in his bed.

He didn't say much. All he wanted to do was look and listen. He didn't think of his aches and pains, or of the close call he had had a few hours before.

His alert eyes were glued on two young men sitting alongside his bed, who were providing better medicine for the injured youth than he could ever get from any doctor. The older of the two was "Pug" Walters, Head Coach of the University Eagles. The other? Star Halfback of the Eagles and potential All-American Dan Danciewitz, better known as "Dancer."

The visit occurred late Wednesday afternoon. Earlier, young Timmy, who's waiting impatiently for his twelfth birthday, had walked all the way from his home at 6212 East Patterson Drive to the University practice field with some friends. The Eagles had an intrasquad scrimmage on tap, the last before Saturday's season opener, and Timmy didn't want to miss it.

"I love football," Timmy told Pug and Dancer in a slow, shy voice. "I'd do anything just to watch a game— even a scrimmage."

Timmy had watched a good part of the scrimmage, standing along the sideline with his friends. But still he had been a little disappointed. Dancer had not yet appeared.

Head Coach Walters didn't want to risk Dancer unnecessarily in a scrimmage. Finally he sent his star halfback in midway through the third period.

Dancer hustled eagerly onto the field, chafing at the

bit from having to sit out the whole first half. The crowd
recognized the familiar grace and lightness of step that
has already made Dancer, still a sophomore and yet
to play his first varsity game, one of the finest breakaway
ballcarriers in the country. They knew he had broken
every freshman record on the books for yards gained and
touchdowns scored, and they cheered, and little Timmy
Rending cheered loudest of all.

At last he would be able to see his hero in action.

He didn't have to wait long. Dancer took a punt on his
own fifteen and moved up the field, slipping away from
tacklers, changing speed, changing direction, feinting
men out of position.

Young Timmy was shouting encouragement along
with the rest of the crowd.

At the midfield stripe, Dancer cut to the right sideline
and turned on his phenomenal speed. For a moment he
was in the clear and it looked as if he might go all the
way. But Sam Christopher, who had kicked the punt, had
dropped back as a safety, and appeared to have Dancer
boxed in. Even though it was only a scrimmage, Dancer
was playing all out. He dived forward at the last minute
to pick up a few extra yards.

He aimed for the sideline. He didn't see the kids standing there cheering him on, and the kids didn't have time
to get out of the way. Dancer hit one of the boys at the
knees and flipped him up into the air.

The boy was Timmy Rending.

It took Timmy a few minutes to get his bearings, and
by that time Head Coach Walters and Dancer were leaning worriedly over him.

"Is he all right? Is he all right?" a deeply concerned
Pug Walters kept asking as Trainer Phil Lichey looked
the boy over.

"Gee, the poor kid," Dancer said, shaking his head. His face was pale, fearful. "I sure hope I didn't hurt him. I didn't even see him standing there."

But to the heartfelt relief of all concerned, young Timmy Rending was all right. The accident had narrowly missed being a real tragedy.

Pug Walters arranged to have Timmy taken home, and the scrimmage resumed. But at least two people had trouble concentrating on it. Pug Walters and Dan Danciewitz couldn't get the little guy out of their thoughts. He had taken his lumps without a whimper, and his spunky performance had captured their hearts.

"When that boy's ready for college," Pug said, "I'd sure love to see him on my squad. He's a fighter all the way."

After practice they decided to drop over to see the boy, to make sure he was all right and to cheer him up a bit.

Little Timmy had been happy to see his hero on the field, but he was both stunned and overjoyed to see him —along with Head Coach Walters—walk into his modest bedroom and ask how he was feeling.

Timmy was feeling all right. In fact, he was feeling just fine—now.

The three of them talked about their favorite subject: football.

"Yes, I think we're going to have a fine team this year," Pug answered to Timmy's interested questioning. "And I think Dancer here is going to lead the way."

Dancer smiled modestly and looked down at the floor. "Don't listen to him, Timmy," he protested. "We've got a fine club all around. We've got a whole team full of stars."

"Gee, I sure do love to watch you run, Mr. Danciewitz," Timmy said slowly and shyly.

"You can just call me Dancer like everyone else,
Timmy . . ."

I skimmed through the rest of the paper on my second
cup of coffee. One thing about feeling that you have things
under control, which was how I always felt, is that a lot of
things don't really interest you. Everybody worries about
the atom bomb and the hydrogen bomb and everything,
but somehow I have the feeling that it won't ever be
dropped quite where I am. I accept the bad logic of this
and wouldn't want to argue it, but that's how I feel. Maybe
it comes from working on newspapers; something about
handling news all the time that convinces you you'll never
be part of it. No reporter really believes his own name
will ever make the obituary column.

I got into newspaper work more or less by accident. My
high school class was on one of those spring tours of Washington when I got tired of holding hands with the horsey-
faced girl who was my partner in line and listening to
talks from guides about the grain of the paper on which the
Declaration of Independence was written. I slipped off and
decided out of nowhere to try the Russian Embassy. I've
always looked old for my age, and so I told them I was a
reporter for the *Harvard Crimson*. They didn't ask for my
cards or anything, and politely showed me all over the
place. It was really sort of interesting. I was going to write
it up for my school paper, but I decided it was too good for
them and sent it off to the *Christian Science Monitor*. They
printed the thing and even paid me twenty dollars for it.
It's amazing how many things I did and how many places
I got into after that by saying I was a reporter for some
paper or other. I used to sell my stuff, too, to different pa-

pers, and between that and telling people all the time that I was a newspaperman, I sort of eased into the profession.

But in sports writing, once around the seasons is enough. When it's spring again and you have to face another 154 games of writing, "Blakeswine rapped a bingle to center and romped home with the tying run on Winston's two-base knock to left," you know you've had it. Bladder writing, my old English teacher Mr. Manquero calls it. One time, after my early enthusiasm had been replaced by a youthful iconoclasm—as if I were the first guy to discover these things—I started collecting all the sports clichés I could find, for a book, to be entitled *The Game Is Never Over Till the Last Man Is Out*. But my period of active social protest was brief. Satirizing is fun only when you like the victim, or at least respect it or him. Besides, clichés aren't the core; they're just part of the bladder business. The real rotten core of sports writing is that you're paid to make believe that the grown men reading you are kids and that the kids they're reading about are gods.

And it's not just sports writing. About 90 per cent of the papers in this country are phony, and don't even care. The other 10 per cent try to be honest occasionally, and occasionally even succeed, but in general the Free American Press is about the greatest hoax in history. A hundred million people are being fooled every day into thinking that they're reading news, that they can find news somewhere among the comic strips and the bra ads and the baseball standings, and that's an awful lot of fooling. Of course, it's not fair just picking on newspapers; there's always the doctors and the druggists, too, and the goddamn garage mechanics. Whenever somebody knows they know more about something than you do, they're probably giving you the works. Just try five different drugstores some day asking for paregoric, for instance, and see what they tell you The

Law says. You'd never believe they were talking about the
same law. And if you try to buy something, and they can
make more money selling you something almost like it,
they'll just tell you that selling the first thing is against
The Law. I've worked in drugstores; I know. I almost die
every time I see one of those ads with some white-jacketed
male model snow-jobbing you about how Your Pharmacist is the noblest public servant since G. Washington. Although chances are he's no worse than the next business-
man, he's certainly no better. What gets me is the way the
druggists are always spending millions of dollars telling
everybody how ethical and sincere they are. It's like *Time*
telling you what a great news magazine it is. Now *Time's*
all right, and I'm sure the druggists don't make a practice
of killing off people by selling them germ pills, but *Time*
sure isn't a *news* magazine, and your Friendly Pharmacist
sure isn't anybody's Public Servant.

I finished my coffee and went upstairs. Everyone was still
asleep; sometimes I'm convinced if I didn't start typing at
eight they'd all sleep till noon. I had planned to knock off
the feature Andy wanted, but then remembered my Royal
Kings report and got to work on that. I gave them the
figures they wanted on Royal Kings sales in the Union and
the drugstores around school and then typed out my Report of Activities and Plans for Future Promotions:

The sales of Royal Kings have receded, as indicated
by the accompanying figures, from the unprecedented
highs of last June. The reason, of course, is the absence
of a large number of students over the summer. You will
note, however, that the figures this year are CONSIDER-
ABLY HIGHER than last September's. I feel confident
my work has had some lasting effect on the smoking hab-
its not only of the student body but *of the faculty and*

townspeople as well! Royal Kings, I am sure, shall long remain the leading cigarette in the vital University consumption area of Midland.

It is good to be back at the helm again, and I am eager to get started. I have already blocked out plans for the Name the Mystery Man Contest, which will run weekly in the *Eagle's Nest.* Several fraternities have promised to feature Royal Kings at their annual smokers. Six local doctors and dentists (as you see, I do not limit my definition of the "University consumption area" to students and faculty alone), along with three campus deans, have agreed to use our Royal King waiting-room display-and-sample cases in their offices. The Student Union has hung our red and blue banner over the cigarette machine, and has agreed to give us *three* of the twelve slots, MORE THAN ANY OTHER BRAND! All nearby drugstores, of course, proudly feature our display items, as they did last year.

I respectfully hope that the above meets with your approval. I feel confident that my activity and sincerity in promoting the uniquely satisfying qualities of Royal Kings will continue to pay substantial dividends to the company. I AM SURE I WILL AGAIN HAVE MUCH GOOD NEWS TO REPORT THIS YEAR!

JACK WYANT
Campus Representative

P.S. I would more than welcome a visit at any time from Mr. Davidson, as mentioned in your letter. Sometime later in the year, as you suggest, would be fine, as my over-all program would be well under way by that time.

Actually, the last thing in the world I wanted was a visit from Mr. Davidson, or anyone else connected with Royal Kings. All I ever did for them was make out ingeniously fictitious reports and trade in all the Royal Kings they sent me for Lords. They sent tons of them, which I was supposed to "distribute liberally among style leaders on campus, preferably two or three cigarettes at a time, while commenting in a casual and friendly fashion about their taste, freshness, popularity, etc." (*So Now You're Working for Royal Kings: A Handbook for Student Representatives,* page 3.) But I liked Lords better myself, and since I couldn't possibly smoke all I got, I enjoyed screwing the company by passing around a competitor's product. They were always hinting about sending someone, but never did.

It was after eight when I finished the report. Some of the other guys were stirring, and when the phone rang in the hall I let one of them answer it. It turned out to be for me anyhow.

"Jackie boy!—Benny—Benny Johnson."

"Yes, sir," I said. I knew it was him right away because he shouted louder than anyone else and was the only one who called me Jackie boy.

"Did Pug talk to you yesterday? Did he get everything straight?"

"Yes, sir." Benny was one of those successful businessmen who can't believe anyone else can ever get anything straight.

"Then I assume you were on the job last night."

"Yes, sir. From now on, sir, I'm on the job twenty-four hours a day."

"How did everything go last night?"

"It went fine, sir."

"I see. Well, that's certainly good news. Yes, sir. If you're sure of it. Are you?"

"Yes, sir."

"Positive?"

"Yes, sir, I am. I'm positive everything went fine."

"Before or after the knife fight?"

I waited a moment. "Excuse me, sir?"

"I hear Dancer got in a knife fight at Smoky's. Isn't that something now, Jackie boy?"

"Who told you that, sir?"

"The bartender."

"I think maybe he was mistaken, sir."

"I don't pay him to be mistaken."

I waited again. "I thought you were paying me to keep an eye on things, sir. If you're going to be paying other people to keep an eye on me—or him—or both of us, I'd just as soon not have the job."

"Very noble and touching, Jackie boy, but I only pay Dutch to tend bar. I own a piece of Smoky's, you know."

"I didn't know."

"A lot of people don't, and I prefer it that way. It's only a little piece, anyhow. But what's with this knife fight business? I have been known to worry about things like that. Worry is very bad for the system, Jackie boy."

"I can't possibly be with Dancer every hour of the day and night. You don't expect that, I'm sure. But I *can* say that Dancer has never in his life gotten into a fight, any kind of fight, let alone a knife fight. He's not that sort."

"But was he in one last night?"

"Did Dutch say absolutely that it was Dancer? Beyond a shadow of a doubt? I'd like to know, frankly, whether we can trust this man or not."

"He sounded pretty damn sure of himself when he spoke to me."

"Ah, hah! Sure of himself, yes. Confident, perhaps. But positive? No. Not positive. Dutch is, I admit, a very good bartender, which is fine, since that's what you're paying him to be. But since you're paying me to keep an eye on Dan, I can tell you positively that he was in his room last night, with me."

"He sure as hell had better been. I called you first to

give you a chance to say your piece. I'll do a little further checking now, if you don't mind."

"Not at all, sir."

"That's the spirit. And you be careful with him, now. We don't want me doing a lot of worrying, do we?"

"No, sir. And no need, sir. In fact, I'm on my way over right now to bid the boy good morning and make sure everything is just fine—which I'm sure it is."

"You do that. Look, I don't want to talk dollars and cents on the phone, but if my checking turns out okay I'll be seeing you around."

"I leave that completely in your hands, sir. In things like this, I feel mutual trust is necessary."

"All right, Jackie boy, cut the bullshit."

When I hung up, I found Harry Giffling leaning against the wall behind me.

"Did you miss anything?"

"I was very careful not to eavesdrop," he said, stepping forward and touching my sleeve. "I just wanted to catch you before you ran off to wherever it is you're always running off to. The Supreme Council met last night and decided to—"

"How could they meet without me? I'm a member."

"You *were* a member, last year, until you were automatically dropped according to the by-laws for missing five meetings in a row without excuse."

"I had excuses."

"Anyhow, we met last night and voted that all Brothers be obliged to undertake a full share of the duties and responsibilities of Brotherhood. Naturally, this was not aimed at any individual Brothers, and of course no individuals were mentioned, but it will mean—"

"Look, Giff, I gotta run now. Can we go over this together later?"

"There's nothing to go over. I just wanted to make sure you understood the implications of—"

"I understand the implications perfectly. Thanks a lot for taking the time to keep me up to date."

I hurried out and headed for Ape Hall, while Giffling, who had followed me to the door, stood on the porch and watched. One of the funny things about me and college was that I didn't quite make it with anybody. Giffling and the guys at the House were always giving me talks about fitting in, and the profs lectured me about becoming serious and trying harder, and the football players, who I liked best of all in some ways, never felt really comfortable with me, because I guess I represented the other half of them. Somehow, everybody always seemed to feel I represented the other half.

What made it all even funnier was that my parents back in the Bronx thought I was doing so damn well. They were really pretty proud of me, because I told them I had a full-tuition, all-expense academic scholarship. They thought that was just marvelous. It fit right in with all their American ideals, which no one ever had more of than my mother and father. It was my father's passion, and my mother, who isn't as passionate about abstractions as she is about the price of groceries, nevertheless absorbed some of his convictions after having to listen to him spout them at her for most of her life. And he spouted them with what I must admit, for a Parks Guard in Crotona Park, was a good deal of rhetorical flourish, most of which he picked up from the codgers who sat around on benches and philosophized at him as he went by with his pointed stick and his burlap bag, in his dark green uniform with a maple leaf Department of Parks shoulder patch.

Basically, my father's difficulties stem from honesty. He is absolutely, unequivocally honest. He is probably the only man in the history of the New York City Department of Parks to turn in every single thing he ever found on his beat. The other guards built up impressive collections of watches and wallets and rings and stuff like that—to say nothing of the money they found and kept—but my father turned in everything, including the money, including even soiled handkerchiefs. This impressed me tremendously when I was a kid, and impresses me that much more now. But my father somehow decided that since he was honest, everyone was honest. One step leads to another once you start down the fateful road, and it wasn't long before my father discovered idealism. He came over to this country from Italy (my name is really Wyamo; too much like a cross between a sparsely settled state and a kitchen cleanser, so I changed it to Wyant) when he was still pretty young, and he went to all those night classes in English and Democracy and everything, and since he's really pretty bright, he could have used his brains and what he learned to make something of himself here, if only he would have wised up a little along the way. But I think he felt that it was God Himself who handed him his stick and burlap bag and put that gold-stitched maple leaf on his shoulder, and that it wasn't his place to question His will. So he stayed there, probably over the years spearing and carrying off as many long tons of chewing-gum wrappers as any man in the country, all the while filling his mind with the kind of gibberish spouted at American Legion rallies on the Fourth of July. The only difference was that he believed in it, and still does, and doesn't have any particular desire to use it to get anything for himself, which distinguishes him from most Legionnaires. He was the kind of immigrant you read about, who came here full of hope and idealism, who felt the lure of America reaching a little deeper than his pocketbook, who not only didn't lose his idealism after getting here but actually gained more of it.

And what did it get him? It got him twenty-five years of

walking through the greens of Crotona Park with a pointed stick in his hand and a bag on his shoulder, dreaming of Jefferson and Lincoln while the kids going by yelled *Wop!* It got him the opportunity of supporting a family on the wonderful abstractions of democratic theory, accompanied by a democratically concrete lack of enough food or clothes or apartments without roaches to let anyone feel like a human being. It got him a beautiful succession of snotty landlords and bill collectors and grocery store clerks. But most of all it got him the wrong end of his own beloved stick.

It was all right, though: he never got sore, he had Abe and Tom and all the rest of his new-found friends to console him. But I got sore. When I started thinking about all this, I got sore, and at him. I blamed him for everything.

And that's how we got into our first and last real fight. "Sure, this is America," I told him. "Where there's money to be made, for everyone—only you gotta go out and scrap for it. Maybe back in Italy a guy who's got a steady job picking up papers is doing okay, but here that's not exactly the dream most people grow up on, including me. You got your America, and I got mine, and God's on the side of mine, like Mr. Lincoln used to say, because he made so many people here like me."

This was in high school, when he found out I was working as a runner for a bookie down the block. But it was a short argument, and after that we never discussed our ideals again. I stopped telling them how I made money, or else told them what I knew they liked to hear, the kind of wild fantasies it takes to keep an idealist happy—like me getting a three-thousand-dollar academic scholarship—and the kind that only an idealist would believe.

But I realized after a while it wasn't his fault. He was just a decent, honest *paisan* who didn't ask anything for himself or hurt anyone or bother anyone, and who was happy enough with the hand-me-down clothes and the landlords and the kids yelling *Wop!* But me, I wanted to get somewhere, I didn't want to become one of the walking statues in Crotona Park. Sure, it's easy enough to say I lacked humility or a sense of dedication or some damn thing (but not honesty: I still had a good deal of that then, and found it very valuable), yet how many people *do* want to spend their lives spearing paper? Let's face it, my father was an exception, and I didn't want to be. Not that kind. I did a lot of thinking and figuring out at this time, and came to certain obvious conclusions. The world was carefully set up so that for little Jack Wyamo, who had some brains and a certain amount of initiative but who was hampered by having an honest and contented father, the only way to get something more than brown roaches out of life was to learn the tricks of the crowd that didn't have roaches. So I studied them, in a general way (nothing I've since seen at firsthand has altered my original findings; Benny Johnson, for instance), but with considerable thoroughness. I looked around me. I read a lot, I asked myself basic questions.

Now, the things these people had—the cars, houses, jobs, degrees, the advantage of people scraping to them and saying *sir*, which I don't think anyone ever said to my father in his life except me—were not necessarily the most important things I wanted. But I sure enough wanted them, *along with* whatever else I would eventually decide I wanted. After all, if every other bubblehead could have them, why couldn't I? Why at least couldn't I have some of them? Why at least couldn't I go to a goddamn college if I wanted to?

I could, I decided, and would.

So I looked—at the businessmen, the newspaper owners, the doctors and lawyers and druggists, the TV and movie stars, the ballplayers, the labor leaders, the politicians, the bank presidents and stock exchange jokers, the generals. The pattern was a convincing one. And so somewhere along the line, not at any given moment, but gradually and diligently, Jack Wyamo, dumb wop, transformed himself body and soul into Jack Wyant, shrewd American—and learned that he had been most fortunately endowed with the knack of doing very well the kind of thing that this great country values so highly, and rewards with such casual but undeniable munificence.

The transformation, of course, was not particularly noted by the world at large. It was too commonplace. Just one more man getting on the trolley.

It was about twenty to nine when I got over to Ape Hall. Dan was reading *Life* magazine.

"Almost time for practice," I said.

"Few minutes," he said, still looking at the magazine. He considered *Life* the intellectual highwater mark of American journalism and read it all the time to help improve his mind. It probably did.

"How you feeling?" I asked, but didn't wait for an answer, because he didn't usually answer questions like that. "Did you see Andy's exceptionally fine column on you visiting that boy yesterday?"

"No."

"You oughta read more about yourself. Modesty is grossly undervalued in most places."

He shrugged. Then he knitted his brows. He moved from thought to thought rather ponderously. "Andy wasn't even there."

"He doesn't say he was. What counter does your girl friend work at? I have to run downtown and I thought if I saw her or something I—"

"Stationery—you know, pencils and notebooks and stuff.

But she ain't there now. She works from noon until nine at night. It's a crummy job."

"I'll keep an eye out for her next time, then."

Dan got up and put on his sweater. "I'm going to practice."

"I'll drop by later. By the way, if anyone says anything about a fight last night, you were here in the dorm with me. The bartender there's been shooting his mouth off, so make it sound convincing. Does the guy know you well?"

"Who?"

"The bartender. Dutch."

"I don't know. It was the first time we ever been there."

"He probably just thinks he recognized you from your pictures. Clearly, he was mistaken. Come, let's go."

I went downstairs with him, wished him a good practice, and then walked back to the House. Every day now it seemed there were more students on campus. I didn't go into the House, because I knew Giffling would be around playing Worthy Supreme Master. Ducking through the hole in the juniper hedges, I found a couple of kids I never saw before raking leaves in the back yard.

"Change in pledge duty for today," I said, offering each a cigarette from a fresh pack of Lords. "Either of you have a car?"

I don't think they remembered ever seeing me before, either, but pledges are easily impressed and the skinny one with freckles said, "I got a car." The other kid was lighting our cigarettes.

"Fine," I said. "Important House business in town."

"They told us to rake up the leaves here."

"Did you look at today's duty roster?"

"Yes, sir."

"Whose name was listed for pledge supervision?"

"Wyant."

"Jack Wyant," I said. "I am Jack Wyant."

"I'm sorry, sir. I didn't realize."

"Let's go."

We went through the hole in the hedge and around to the parking lot.

"That's mine over there."

It was a 1960 Dodge convertible, red with cream interior. Most of the cars were new; all were shiny. If you let your car get too dirty, the brothers printed WASH with their fingers in the dust. We got in and I said, "I have to see the mayor about something. Take Third down to Chester and then cut right five blocks to City Hall. Put the top down; it's warm."

He let me off at City Hall.

"How will you get back?"

"I'll manage." I gave him a pack of Lords and he drove off, pushing the button on his dash to make the top go back up. When he was out of sight, I walked across the street and around the corner to the YWCA. I asked the gray old lady standing in front of the mail slots at the desk if I could see Miss Steiner. "I'm her uncle," I said.

She viewed me suspiciously.

"Many uncles are hardly older than their nieces or nephews, as the case may be. It's quite common, really."

"I'll ring Miss Steiner. You can speak to her on the house phone. Over there."

The house phone was near the doorway to what they probably called the Friendship Room. There were leather couches bulging grotesquely and tearing at the arms, and wooden chairs, and a ping-pong table in the middle. There was also a piano with one broken caster leaning against the wall and some *Reader's Digests* lying around. No one was there, and the room smelled like homesick waifs in damp cellars. I had never been in a YWCA before, but I could picture the upstairs rooms with their single iron beds and their bureaus with Bibles on top and the veneer peeling off, with pale bespectacled girls doing their ironing and writing letters back home and putting their stringy hair up in old-fashioned curlers; I could see them at night lying stiffly under their flat virginal counterpanes, staring blankly at the paint coming off the ceiling and dreaming of things romantic and beautiful and far off, while in the background the radiator hissed.

"Hello, who is this? I have no uncle."

"Well, Dan told me everything else except whether or not you had any uncles, so I thought I'd find out by—"

"Who is this?"

"Jack Wyant."

"Oh."

"I take it Dan's mentioned me?"

"I may have you confused with someone else."

"May I come up?"

"You're not allowed. I'll be down."

I sat on one of the couches facing the ping-pong table and read about menopausal frigidity in a tattered *Digest*. The couch received me voluptuously up to the armpits, and I had to struggle getting out to greet May. She was pretty short. Her hair was a sort of colorless brown, with the required YWCA look of the inverted bowl. Her figure was all right though.

"How do you do?" I said.

"What do you want?"

Everything in her face looked clenched, as if she was afraid to let anything go, and I had the feeling that if she didn't want to let go, she wouldn't. The only really interesting thing in her face was the pug nose.

"I was on my way to City Hall and thought I'd drop in and say hello. Dan was telling me all about you last night and I—"

"Except my uncles. Were you there when he came back? Was there a fight?"

"I happened to be passing by. The other guy had a knife."

"Oh . . ."

"But he also had a bloodied nose. Whereas Dan was quite untouched. We got Dan out of there before the cops came."

"We?"

"I."

"I see. I told Dan not to go back. The fellow was drunk anyhow, and I didn't care what he said."

"What did he say?"

"Nothing. The usual junk. But Dan insisted on being noble. What makes men think they have to be noble?"

"Perhaps Dan is just inherently noble. It'd be a good idea if you two stayed away from Smoky's. The bartender's got a big mouth and the coach wouldn't like hearing about fights and such."

"I don't think Dan cares what the coach hears."

"What about the dean?"

She shrugged. "All right. We'll stay away."

We were still standing, between the couch and the ping-pong table. "One other thing: he says you were telling him he ought to do more of his own work this year."

"That was his idea."

"But you encouraged it."

"Of course I encouraged it. He's never going to learn anything with you doing his work for him."

"How long have you known Dan?"

"A few weeks. Since he got back."

"I know love is blind and everything, but have you ever discussed history with him, or chemistry, or the English sentence? He has some rather remarkable theories on the English sentence."

"Of course he's no genius, as he insists you are. But he wants to learn, and he'll try hard. He should have the chance to make it on his own."

"Dan looks intelligent, and even sounds intelligent, but behind those clear blue eyes there lurks something less than an intelligent mind."

"He's not stupid."

"Leave us not quibble. I've worked with Dan for a year now, and I'm quite familiar with his capacities, or lack thereof. If you push this independence business too far, you'll flunk him out. He won't make it on his own. He can't."

She said nothing to that.

"And if I'm going to be the one to help him," I went on, "I'd like to do it my own way."

"I don't like the way you talk about Dan."

"I try to be honest," I said. "It's been nice meeting you. I'm sure we'll bump into each other again." I waited a moment, then said, "You know, a passionate love affair is not the best way of keeping in shape for football. An awful lot of people would be disappointed if Dan didn't do as well as he's expected to do."

"I wouldn't. He wouldn't."

"But we shouldn't be selfish in these things, should we? And you know, Dan is impressively virgin. Treat him gently."

"Any other advice?"

"Follow your conscience," I said. "I've always found that best."

CHAPTER SEVEN

It was already ten-thirty when I bade good day to the gray old lady in front of the mail slots, and since I had to be downtown for the Townbird luncheon, I walked a few blocks to the *Standard* office and got to work on my feature. No one was around; most people work nights on a morning paper.

The eight or ten features I had already done on Dancer had probably made him the most written-about freshman in the country last year. He certainly got more publicity than anybody on our varsity. I had told about his childhood heroes. I told of the high school coach convincing him to try out for the team, convincing him that he was good enough. I told of his high school feats, his records. I analyzed his style of play, gave his measurements, told how fast he could run the 100 both in and out of uniform. I told of his father working in the sooty coal mines, of his mother taking in laundry. I quoted Dancer and his parents on the great democratic virtues of athletic scholarships, which were given without favor to rich and poor alike, to white man and black, and even to sons of Polish coal miners.

Andy faithfully sent all the stories out on the wire, because he was determined that we were going to have an All-American in Dancer. A surprising number of them—

considering that Dan was still a freshman—were picked up around the state, and even in places like Chicago, which shows how well Andy did his work. Everywhere he went, with every editor he met, he plugged Dancer. This, of course, is how All-Americans are made, by editors, by press agents. Andy had it all figured out: honorable mention or possibly third team this year, and then second team, and then first. The University had not had anything resembling an All-American in ten years, and Dan was too good a possibility to leave to chance.

Besides, Andy was the guy who put the school onto Dancer, and he never let anyone forget it. Some old friend of his ran a little paper in Pennsylvania and passed the word along to him, and he passed it on to Pug, who sent out Red Warwick to scout Dancer in a couple of games. A lot of big-name high school stars look good only because the guys they play against, or with, are so bad. If a team only has one decent runner, he runs on practically every play and can build up some pretty impressive statistics. Pug didn't care how many touchdowns Dan had made, or how many thousands of yards he had gained; he wanted to know if he could hold onto a ball, if he had balance, if he had good movement and strong acceleration, if he could cut, if he had lateral speed, if he was big enough and tough enough to make it in college. A lot of high school speedsters are what Pug calls track stars: 160-pounders who shy away from tacklers and whose fine fragile bones break like china the first time a really big college lineman muscles in on them.

Warwick went and watched and came back and said that Dancer could do everything a split-T halfback could be expected to do, could even pass, so that we could use him on the halfback option. He said he was strong going into the line, had great drive in his legs, charged tacklers even in midfield, and had perfect movements and great speed in every direction. Pug told Warwick to get him. Of course, at least thirty or forty other colleges were after Dancer, but Red did a great job approaching him and his parents, and for a while it looked as if we had him. And then one night Pug got a desperate long-distance call. Three other schools were outbidding us, and the father, who had seemed to be on our side, was wavering.

Those remarkable published histories of our great universities (usually called something like *A Light on the Hill* or *Beacon in the Desert*) make much of turning points, of the year the president expanded the science departments, or the time a brilliant sociologist joined the faculty and brought the best graduate students in the country with him. But the real turning points don't get in the histories. These are the ones precipitated by hectic midnight phone calls from some hick town in the hills of Pennsylvania.

Four men went to see President Irvine the next morning: Pug; Bob Stanley, our athletic director; Andy Rivers; and Benny Johnson. Pug did not want Benny along. He hated Benny, and so did Bob Stanley, and so did President Irvine. But Benny had the real money and the real noise of the alumni behind him, and Bob Stanley, who was cooler and more businesslike than Pug, insisted on bringing Benny in on it.

The meeting took place within a historical perspective familiar to all men present. Ten years before, when Ralph Irvine moved up through the English department and the deanship to become president, the University was really big time in football. Irvine knew he could never beat the Townbirds and the Bennys head-on, and instead worked on a quiet, step-by-step de-emphasis of athletics, especially football. He hoped to cover up the decline by carefully planned scheduling, gradually replacing tough opponents with weaker ones, so that the team—and the money it

cost—could wither away by stages without the University
ever having a disastrous season. Only the plan didn't work.
The team fell apart instantly, and we had one bad season
after another. Irvine even changed coaches a couple of
times—at the prodding of the Townbirds—but it never
made any difference. We just kept losing, and nobody but
the English Department seemed happy. Pressure from the
students and the alumni and the Townbirds and the legis-
lators and the governor got pretty heavy. Irvine just
couldn't buck it alone. He fought them almost to a stand-
still for a year or so, even gave speeches throughout the
state to alumni groups, but he couldn't manage to get anyone excited enough about the growing fame and brilliance
of our faculty to make them forget the ineptitude of our
defensive tackles. Finally he had to admit he was beaten.

He started back up the painful road he had just come
down, and gradually more and more money went into the
team. The money did not come fast enough, though, and
as the team got better, the schedule perversely got tougher,
so that the team that lost going down also lost coming up.
Another coach got the boot and Pug was brought in and
given what he thought was a blank check. But President Irvine, as Pug and Andy and Benny soon realized, still didn't
have his heart in it, and everything had come to a head at
that early morning meeting.

Pug presented their case: they needed more scholarships, and especially more free rides, because partial scholarships no longer got anyone worth getting. But even that
was not enough. All schools had full scholarships, and if
you really wanted someone, someone like Dancer, you had
to have something more to offer, more fringes, more in-
direct help from alumni in general and from the Townbirds in particular. Such aid was of course forbidden by
the NCAA, and Irvine pointed this out, as he had many
times before. He said that the University could not con-

done extravagant scholarship aid or illegal fringes, and that if the football team were to prosper, it would have to do so within clear-cut legal and moral bounds. His eloquence, from what I later pieced together from Andy and Pug, produced a rather moving plea.

Benny, however, was unmoved. He gave Irvine, the former English teacher, the Robert Burns scholar, the man who spent twenty years studying and teaching Romantic literature of the nineteenth century, the word about realistic life in the twentieth century. The alumni were sick and tired of mealy-mouthed excuses. They wanted a team, a good team, and they wanted one soon. Irvine had promised to help Pug, and they were now calling in that promise. Everyone knew all the other schools cut corners, and the only way to get anywhere would be to cut along with them. This was not a literary tea; this was big-time football, big business, and in business when the other guy hedges, you hedge too—and if you're real smart you even do a little hedging ahead of time, before the other guy beats you to it.

The meeting lasted about an hour, and the second half of that hour was taken up by Benny's lecture on the inverse relationship between morality and business success, and at the end of the meeting Pug called Red Warwick in Humbolt, Pennsylvania, and two hours later we had Dan sewed up. We got Dan by giving him a free-ride scholarship worth ten or twelve thousand dollars over a four-year period, and a few extras. The extras included a new Chevrolet for his father, courtesy of an alumnus who owned a Pennsylvania Chevrolet agency, plus a promise of future free-ride no-strings-attached scholarships for Dan's younger brother (who already showed some football promise) and sister (who did not), plus a promise of both a summer job for Dan near his home and a fake part-time job around campus—both paying well above the going rate. Thus it was easy to see why Pug and Benny wanted someone to keep tabs on Dan: in the final cold dollars-and-cents estimate, he was the most valuable man on the squad, representing a total investment of about thirty thousand dollars.

Of course, I never wrote a feature about that, and did not do so that morning in the *Standard* office. Instead I wrote a very impressive piece—and, at least in part, a surprisingly truthful one—about Dan's great inner hunger for education. Here, I said, is not someone who thinks only of football, much as he loves the sport. Here is a serious young man preparing himself to be a trained and useful citizen—trying to decide between accountancy and engineering, even giving thought to theoretical physics. Here again we can see the many ways in which the great American sport of football supports the educational objectives of our great universities to produce for America the leadership we need to stay ahead of the Russians in our modern, troubled times.

I finished at about eleven-thirty and put the story on Andy's desk under a pack of Lords. The two non-glass walls of his office were covered with pictures of Andy with famous athletes; he'd go to these meetings and conventions in Chicago and places like that and shove in next to Gene Tunney or Johnny Unitas or Willie Mays or somebody, and then send the photos to them to be autographed. He also had a whole bunch of his columns framed: COACH SAYS TASK IS MOLDING YOUTH, NOT WINNING GAMES. COMPETITIVE SPORTS STRENGTHEN MORAL FIBER, EDUCATOR SAYS. COACH STRESSES GUTS, GOD.

His picture ran with the column every day, and that was the biggest fraud of all. Andy went on a diet before they took it, the one great diet of his life, then had them take around twenty shots, and then picked the best one of those, and *then* had someone touch that one up. This was fifteen years ago, and he was still using it. For someone whose face was in the paper every day, it was amazing how easily Andy traveled around Midland without ever being recognized.

Don Ames had drifted into the office and was reading *Nugget* magazine as I emerged. When the phone rang, he said: "Take it, will you? I'm busy."

"I gotta get over to the Townbirds."

"Go on, you work here too."

I knew damn well what it'd be.

"Say, hello there . . . I was wondering could you tell me the year DiMaggio hit in all those games straight, and how many it was."

People are always calling newspapers for things like that, and you're supposed to answer everything. Sometimes it takes hours to look up some of the stuff, but it's part of serving the public.

"Fifty-one games in 1939," I said, and hung up.

"Fifty-six in '41," Don Ames said, without raising his eyes.

"I knew it was something like that," I agreed as I left. What the hell difference did it make? If that's all someone had to worry about in the world, his life must be pretty cushy.

Most of the Townbirds were still at the bar when I got to the Midland Hotel about a quarter to twelve. I rode the elevator up to the banquet room, took my regular place at the back table, and started working on the story, writing it out by hand. A few Birds drifted in early and talked together up front. The waiters hurried around with their little metal carts, setting up the tables.

I worked up a lead on the Townbirds pledging full support to the University and the team on the eve of the new season, and quoted Benny on the Birds' confidence that this year we would finally come out of the wilderness and into the sunshine. Then I summarized Pug's remarks about

the team's chances and quoted a few pleasantries from
President Irvine. I was about to put it in my pocket when
I remembered the scouting report. I inserted a paragraph
on Pug warning that we would be facing a tough, seasoned,
and well-coached team, with great depth and a dangerous
offense, and would need every break we could get to win.
Ours is essentially a green and inexperienced team, he
reminded the audience, and we would be outweighed both
in the line and in the backfield.

The tables were filling up, and the room had become
pretty noisy. The first requisite for a Townbird was the
inability to talk softly. As usual, everyone was jovial, with a
lot of slapping of backs and shaking of hands. I don't
know what it was, but the Townbirds were almost all short.
I had noticed that before. They were what clothing stores
euphemistically call portlies, and most were as tall at table
as they were standing up.

Everyone stood up and clapped when Benny led Pug,
Andy Rivers, President Irvine, and a lemon-faced minister
to the main table. Benny called the group to order and we
all sang the Alma Mater. After the minister's inspired grace,
everyone cleared his throat and started eating. We had
chicken à la king. We always had chicken à la king.

Seating at the tables was pretty well worked out. Up
front, along with G. A. Magnus, publisher of the *Standard*,
were the bank presidents and the owners of the big department stores. Behind them were the successful real estate
men and the contractors and some of the richer doctors
and the owners of restaurants, hotels, and laundry chains,
followed by the dentists and the guys who ran little
hardware and tobacco stores and things like that. Since
mine was a back table, the seven men with me weren't
much, and I ignored them as they talked football through
the meal with their mouths full of food. I offered Lords
around when we finished, but most of them pulled out

big cigars, which I suspect were more expensive than the ones they smoked when no one was looking.

The meeting itself was pretty dull. Most were, although occasionally things broke into the open. One time an already doomed coach roared back after a long and painful session of harsh questioning ("Why the hell did you pass that time in the fourth period? It was third down and we only had two yards to go and . . .") and spent a half hour telling the stunned Birds how stupid they were and how much more he knew about football then they would ever know. It sounds like a pretty natural thing to do, but so far as I know he's the only coach in the country ever to have done it. Another time a coach said (had he read Homer? I don't know—it's possible, I guess) that if his halfbacks didn't stop fumbling and his team didn't start winning and the Birds didn't stop haunting him, he was going to leave town with a football under his arm and keep walking south until he got down through Texas and into Mexico, and then was going to keep right on walking until somebody stopped him and asked what it was he was carrying under his arm—and then he would settle down.

During the season the Townbirds met once a week—a hundred little awkward fat men sitting around drinking martinis and eating chicken à la king with floury gravy and talking about the lure and challenge and glory of manly athletic endeavor. They always met the Monday after the game until last year, when that got pretty painful, especially for Pug. Week after week he had to face those guys and give them excuses for losing. It was particularly bad last year, because the Birds, who had bent over backwards being understanding during his first year, had really counted on a winning season. Finally, with only two games left and the team sporting a 1–5 record, Benny decided he couldn't take it any more either. He gave a little speech to the boys on the Will to Win as part of the American Way of Life.

"I'm on the road a lot," he told Pug and the Birds, "and you don't *know* what agony I go through facing these guys I meet around—both our own guys and guys from other schools—and have to hear them ask all the time, 'How's it feel to be a loser?' And let me tell you, it feels lousy. I just can't face those guys any more, I tell you. And with that goddamn English teacher of a president we got over there in his ivy tower, if anybody's gonna do anything about letting us know for a change how it feels to be a winner, it's gonna have to be us, you and me. Because as for me, I'm just sick, I tell you—sick at heart. I used to look forward to Saturdays—I looked forward to them when I used to have the honor of going out there myself on the field, and I used to look forward to it for a long time after, when we had good teams and even great teams once in a while. Now I dread Saturdays, because I know I won't be able to sleep that night—and I even dread Mondays now, too, because it just means grinding the salt in a little deeper."

That was when someone suggested moving the meetings up to Thursdays, before the games, so they could at least have a chance to forget the preceding Saturday and think optimistically about the coming one. The idea carried, with the provision, suggested by Benny, that the meetings be moved back to Monday as soon as the situation warranted.

But now with a new season beginning, everyone was everyone's friend again, optimism was rampant, and Benny praised Pug and President Irvine, and they in turn praised him right back.

Irvine, of course, had the hardest time making it sound convincing. He never felt much at home with the Birds, with hardware salesmen and real estate speculators and drugstore owners whose single overriding interest was a game that deep in his heart Irvine thought was just a little silly, and he usually appeared only at the first meeting, which was often enough for all concerned.

He started off with a joke about Daniel in the lion's den that no one laughed at, and then, fighting down his gorge, complimented the Birds and all our faithful alumni for their devoted service to the University. But Irvine could never strike the right note with the Birds, and everyone shuffled uncomfortably when he lumped football in with things like the student newspaper, religious organizations, student government, academic clubs, and research projects. Even when he mentioned the new stadium, which the Birds had been crying for for years, he right away killed off the applause by saying that we also needed new dorms and a new auditorium and new chemistry and humanities buildings.

Quite clearly, Irvine bored the Birds, but they listened spellbound to Pug's scouting report. He warned that we would be outweighed in the line and the backfield and would be facing a rough and seasoned team, with a good coach, and that we would need every break in the game to win. Then he gave them a pretty oversimplified analysis of their offensive and defensive formations and a few comments about their key players. The Birds looked upon themselves as football experts, and they loved the idea of getting the real technical inside scoop. They all looked forward to turning casually to some friend in the stands on Saturday and saying, "Notice how that left tackle commits himself on every play?—Perfect setup for a draw."

The meeting ended with the minister blessing Midland and the University and all the Townbirds and Pug and President Irvine and the whole football team and the Midland Hotel and the dinnerware used at the luncheon.

Everyone got up and stood around shouting at each other or else headed for the main table to talk to the bigwigs. I got through to Andy. "The feature's already on your desk, sir."

"Okay. You going to practice this afternoon?"

"Naturally, sir."

"Did you manage to make it this morning?"

"Yes, sir." I was safe; Andy never made morning practice.

"Okay. Maybe I'll drop by this afternoon."

I started for the door, but then saw President Irvine standing alone near the main table; the portlies were interested only in Benny and Pug. I went over and said hello, and he seemed really glad to see me, probably because I was the only other guy in the room who knew Robert Burns wasn't only a cigar.

"You gave a very good talk, sir."

"Thank you, Jack. I fear I didn't thrill our friends, however."

"I think you did fine, sir."

He laughed, but kind of uncomfortably. I liked Irvine. Even though he was president he still taught the Romantic lit course and I took it from him and he was just fine. He said I was one of the best students he ever had and he was always very friendly. I hated seeing him just standing around with all those Birds elbowing each other in the ribs and everything.

"I throw the sand against the wind," he said, "and the wind throws it back again."

"Blake," I said.

He smiled. "Best right end we ever had."

Benny came over and slapped Irvine on the shoulder. Irvine stiffened.

"Much thanks for stopping by, Ralph," Benny said. "The boys ate it up."

"My pleasure."

Benny was pretty bald, and the baldness made his round face look even rounder. He was about the same height as the rest of the Birds, only a little fatter. "I'm glad you brought up the stadium," he said. "That's a sore point around here, you know. Did you know that we got the smallest stadium of any big-time school in the country?— one of the boys got interested and he looked up the figures. Did you know that, now? You know, when you look second-rate, people start tabbing you as second-rate."

"We're doing our best, of course, to get everything we need. We've been growing so fast that—"

"But don't you see if we get a bigger stadium we can pull in enough money to build all the dorms and classes and stuff you want."

"We're not filling up the stadium we have."

"Because we ain't got a team, Ralph! That's what I keep telling you—these things work together. You give us one, a stadium, and two, a team, and we'll give you all the dorms you want."

"Most schools have found it doesn't work that way."

"Never mind most schools—this is our school. We do things our own way here."

Pug came over and smiled at Irvine. "You listen to Benny now, sir. I always listen when he tells me how to run the football team."

"Very funny, Pug," Benny said. "Only you know the school doesn't *belong* to Ralph—it belongs to everybody, the whole state, and the students and the alumni. We got a voice in things and we expect to use it."

"The football team belongs to everyone too, right, Benny?" Pug said.

"It sure does."

"But only when it wins . . ."

Benny laughed kind of coldly. "I wish it was that way, Pug boy. Unfortunately it belongs to us when you lose too."

"When *I* lose . . ."

"When *we* lose."

"Thank you, Benny."

"Only we're gonna win this year."

"That's right," Pug said.

Benny looked over at me. "If you good people will excuse me, I have a few words with Jackie boy."

He took me off to one side. Irvine watched us go kind of sadly. He liked me. He had hopes for me.

"How's everything going?" Benny asked with that booming whisper he used to discuss matters of importance.

"Fine," I said. "Dan's in great shape. He has a fine attitude toward his studies."

"You bone him up good now—only don't let him knock himself out on the books. He'll have plenty of time to catch up when the season's over."

"We're off to a great start, sir. You should hear him go at his chemistry: H_2O_2 plus $C_{14}H_{12}N_6$ equals—"

"Good, good. Only it's a shame he has to take all that crap."

"I know," I said.

"By the way—I talked to Dutch again."

"Oh? And what did he say?"

"He says maybe he was mistaken. One of the other boys thinks it was a couple of soldiers."

"Perhaps in the future, sir, we ought to listen more to this other guy. I did a little checking, too. One of the soldiers was wearing civvies, and was built something like Dan . . . So I guess that settles that."

He nodded, but sort of sourly. He hated losing an argument. "Here," he growled as he stuffed an envelope in my pocket. "You look later and if you have any complaints you let me know."

"Will it be weekly or monthly?"

"Weekly. Until the season's over."

"But like you said, he'll have a lot of catching up then.

He can just as easily get in trouble or something after the—"

"We'll discuss it when the time comes, Jackie boy. Don't be greedy. It's a very bad thing for people to be greedy."

"My only concern is Dan's welfare."

"Us, too, Jackie boy. We're a pretty noble-minded crowd around here."

"The Birds fly straight and high," I said.

"And you would be a wise young man," he said, thumping his finger on my chest, "not to be standing under us looking up at the wrong time."

CHAPTER EIGHT

I got downstairs about two o'clock and waited outside the revolving door for Pug, who was still up at the luncheon, so I could ride back to practice with him. But then a black Oldsmobile Ninety-Eight swung to the curb and honked.

"Heading back?" President Irvine called over.

"Yes, sir." I hurried around and got in alongside him. "Thank you very much, sir."

He drove for a few minutes in silence, hunched forward over the wheel, holding it carefully with two hands, watching the traffic around him. When we got past the center of town and onto Third Street, he sat back and relaxed a little. He was a very careful guy.

"Enjoy the luncheon?" he said, without taking his eyes off the road.

"The food was unique," I said.

He laughed a little and then was quiet.

"I guess you find them pretty boring, sir," I said.

"On the contrary. The ultimate advantage the educated man has over the boobs—if you'll pardon my lack of modesty—is that he can always find them interesting as studies, whereas they find him a dreadful bore."

"I guess I'm a boob then, sir. I find them pretty dull."

"You don't find the world fascinating enough, Jack. The truly intelligent man is always a child at heart. Everything is new and wonderful—full of wonder—for him. He has a great zest for things."

"Yes, sir," I said. Actually, much as I liked Irvine, I always felt he was better in class than out. A lot of teachers are like that. They do fine plugging zest or teaching ethics or morality or the Good Life as long as they stick to Blake or Shakespeare or even Newton or Charlemagne, because these were pretty zesty guys, but when they get out of class and start talking right *at* these things, it falls a little flat. I think Irvine liked to look upon himself as a captain of the armada in the Great Adventure of Ideas and all that sort of thing, but when you came right down to it, he was just a pretty nice guy who was smart and regular and who had learned a lot more, I think, than I'd really want to learn. Of course, Irvine was not the impractical dreamer the Birds thought he was. He was practical as hell, actually, and a good president, with a pretty good grasp of economics and business affairs. The University had done well under him. The students liked him and the faculty swore by him. He got along well with the governor and managed to wheedle most of the money he needed from the legislature, and also managed, which was more difficult, to get most of it spent on the right things. He was even popular with the alumni and the townspeople and the local businessmen —except for the jockstrap crowd. And even there he could have done well if he wanted to. But Irvine just couldn't bring himself to accept football as an important part of a university program, and he went along with the Birds only as far as he had to, and even that reluctantly.

"That's one of the joys of teaching," he went on. "You never have to stagnate; there's always something new to learn, something to keep your mind alive."

"Yes, sir," I said. Irvine wanted me to become a teacher. He said once if I went on for my doctor's, he would hire me. I told him I would think about it, because I hadn't made up my mind about my life's work. Only I had, at least about teaching. I wasn't going to spend my life trying to cultivate a field of vegetables into memorizing the seven causes of the Civil War. They're too dumb to have to know things like that anyhow, and I'm against putting dangerous things like knowledge into the minds of dumb people. In fact, I'm pretty much against the whole idea of democratic education. I mean the sort of thing you get in state universities, where anybody can come, and is even encouraged to come, and where the whole point is to get as many people as possible through, by dragging them or threatening them or making things easier for them, by doing anything you can possibly do, just as long as you get them *through*. I think that's bad. It's like giving a blind inbecile a machine gun. Besides that, teaching doesn't pay enough. I've seen too many poor slobs living in Quonset huts with three kids crying and a scrawny wife out working somewhere as a waitress for five or ten years so the guy could get his Ph.D. by writing a dissertation on the position of the adverb in Middle English Sermons from 1450 to 1463. No, thank you. And even after you get the degree, then what? You give lectures to whole rooms full of open-mouthed students. You grade papers, and more papers, and more papers. And I know what these papers are like: "The American Civil War was started by President Abreham Lincoln to free the slaves in the South because the nation could not live with one halft its people in chains of slavery he said. The War was very long and bloody and created hard feelings on the part of all concerned. Then all the negros were freed and Lincoln was assinated by an insenced madman, followed by the Industrial Revolution." No, thank you.

"You're the kind of person we've got to get if we're to

survive," Irvine said. "I really mean that—although not just in teaching, because naturally we can't get all the best men. But somehow we've got to get people like yourself into the socially useful occupations—into education, or government, or the arts, or law, medicine, science, journalism, the ministry, or at least into the more responsible areas of business. Because if when we get through with you, all you want to do is make money, we've somehow failed— we've failed you and we've failed our whole civilization. People like you represent the best we have, Jack—intelligence, honesty, toughness of spirit, determination, social awareness. If we consistently lose people like yourself to the money grubbers, then I'm afraid eventually we'll have lost everything."

"That description doesn't sound like me, sir."

"Modest Jack."

"Honest Jack," I said, and he laughed. I laughed a little too.

"Where you you heading?"

"The practice field, sir—but I can walk from wherever you're going."

"No need."

We drove through the main gate of the University, and the campus cop saluted smartly. The campus was pretty crowded, and in front of the dorms the cars were lined solidly—parents' cars, loaded with all the junk junior or sis wanted to take back to school, all the clothes, the pennants, the old dance mementoes, the inscribed beer mugs, the portable record players, the tennis rackets, the pictures of boy friends and girl friends. The fathers were walking back and forth from the open trunks of their cars to the dorms, their arms loaded, their fleshy faces sweating, while the mothers stood to one side, nervous, worrying about the old man straining himself and the daughter getting in trouble. You could see it in their faces. *I know she's a good girl, I*

*know she's always been a good girl, but maybe this year
will be the year* . . .

"A good sight, isn't it?" Irvine said. "The campus coming
to life again, our annual rebirth, our renaissance."

"Yes, sir."

He drove across campus and out the north gate and
stopped in front of the stadium, near the locker-room entrance.

"Do you write all the practice stories?" he asked.

"Yes, sir. Mr. Rivers does the important stuff."

"Yes, I see his byline. I read it all with great interest,
you know."

"I guess a lot of people do, sir."

"How does the team look this year, Jack? Between you
and me."

"Well . . . better than last year, sir."

"That's what everyone said last year. How much better?"

"A lot, I think. Pug's been scouting around all winter,
and he's picked up a lot of junior college transfers. Good
ones. If they come through, we'll be in fine shape."

"What about this Danciewitz boy? Is he as good as Andy
keeps telling us?"

"He's very good, sir. And Pug's been working hard with
him."

"Pug seems to be finding his stride this year, doesn't
he?"

"He just never got the breaks before, sir. The players
swear by him. I think he's going to show people this year."

I did, too. More than that, I really hoped he would. No
one knows better than I what a phony business big-time
football is, but I was pulling as hard as I could for Pug,
for the whole team. Not because I gave a damn for Benny
Johnson and all the fatheaded alums, but because of Pug
himself, and because of Irvine. The only two decent guys
in the whole mess were the ones who'd be hurt most

if the team flopped again, and those were two of the very few guys in the world I didn't want to see hurt.

"I'm sure he's an excellent coach," Irvine said. "Of course, so were the last three we had. By the way—are you working for Benny now? I saw you talking with him, and—"

"For Benny? No, sir. I just run into him a lot; he's very interested in the team."

"You've still got your scholarship, haven't you?"

"Yes, sir. Two hundred dollars a year."

"Do you have any G.I. Bill?"

"No, sir. I've never been in the service."

"And you're tutoring for Pug again?"

"Yes, sir."

"What else do you do?"

"Odds and ends, sir."

"I went through college the same way, you know—picking up a few dollars here, a few there. Of course, it's unfortunate a good student has to do that, but in a way I'm almost glad the free rides all go to the football players, because then in the long run people like you, who have to do it the hard way, are rewarded with a kind of toughening of the moral fiber that the football players never get. I think it really helps, really teaches you something."

"Yes, sir," I said. "I've learned a lot."

Maybe that was why I liked Irvine: his innocence. He really believed in things. Somehow he managed, while struggling for his life in the middle of the several-hundred-million-dollar investment in fakery that a big university stands for—and boy, he really *was* in the middle; he got it from all sides—to keep on believing in the things he had always believed in. Honesty and scholarship and character and the value of education—things like that. That's what I need, I used to tell myself sometimes, to believe in a few things like that. And I tried. I even used Irvine as my model. Why can't you be like him? I used to say to myself.

But I couldn't; I can't. I don't have his innocence. And you need that. Without that, Irvine would have been as fake as everything and everybody else.

"Have you given any thought to the future, Jack?"

"Not too much, sir. I've been more or less taking things as they come."

"It doesn't hurt to look ahead on occasion. It's all right making your way now off the scraps and leavings, but eventually you'll want something more solid. You don't want to end up anybody's toady, Jack."

"No, sir."

"They can get you, you know. That gang downtown. You go along thinking you're putting it over on them, and then you realize that all along they've been putting it over on you. And without even trying. They don't have to try, Jack; they've got enough on their side to get people anyhow, to get them by default. Don't let them get you."

"They won't get me, sir," I said. Then I smiled. "I can't stand chicken à la king."

He laughed a little. Not too much.

"Well, thank you very much for the ride, sir. I'll remember what you said."

"Yes. We'll see you around."

I went through the empty locker room, past the sign that said

IT'S NOT THE SIZE OF DOG IN THE FIGHT

THAT COUNTS

BUT THE SIZE OF THE FIGHT IN THE DOG

and waved to Nick Paglucci, who was sorting out practice shoes and old sweatshirts in the equipment room, the dead stub of his cigar sticking out a quarter-inch further than his dirt-gray mustache. Nick was about fifty, short, and a little fat, with a grayish stubble: Pug said every equipment man he had ever seen, from high school up, looked the same. Nick didn't wave back. They were all grumpy, too, and never talked much, but once they got started they'd go on for hours about their kids and how hard it rained in the spring back in Indiana or wherever they came from. I threw a pack of Lords through the open half of the stablelike door of the equipment room and Nick caught it and snarled a little and went on sorting out the sweatshirts.

I found an empty office down in the catacombs under the gym—Red Warwick's—and used his typewriter to do my practice story. His walls were covered with pictures of teams, too, just like Pug's. I don't think there's a coach in the country who doesn't have a few hundred gray-brown zombies gaping down on him as he works. Then I typed up the Townbird story from my handwritten draft and stuck both stories in my pocket and went out and up the runway to the practice field. Pug was back by this time, up on his usual perch, a ten-foot wooden stand in the center of the field, from which he always watched practice. Pug didn't believe in getting too close to the boys; he thought it was bad to criticize them personally, bad even to compliment them. He organized the practice sessions and then let the assistant coaches run them while he watched everything from his perch, a pair of binoculars around his neck. Once in a while he'd signal something to Piney Savage, who had the offensive backfield, or Joe Minotti, who had the line, or Sam Bassey, who had the ends and the defensive backfield, but most of the time he'd just watch and let them run things themselves. With him on the stand he always had Jerry Dinsmoor, the student manager, who took down notes for Pug in a notebook, as many as five or eight or even ten pages from an hour's practice. Most people watching a practice, or even a game, don't see anything. Pug saw everything, and everything he saw Jerry Dinsmoor put down in the notebook:

Janvers—stance—weight too far forward, ass high
Planton—punt—body sway to left, step too long
Marshall—feed—left elbow away from body
Tensch—reception—bad balance—hands closed, stiff
Washington—pass protection—flatfooted

Every day after practice Pug met with the assistants to go over the notes, telling them what to look for the next day, what to correct, criticize, change; and the next day from his perch Pug would watch to see that the corrections were made, and to look for new mistakes, peering through his binoculars, dictating notes to Jerry Dinsmoor.

The players seldom saw Pug at close range. He made a point of never going in the locker room, for instance, except for a few minutes right before a game, when he would speak to the team, more a series of instructions and directions than a pep talk, but which because of the rarity of his appearances carried as much emotional force for the kids as a real Rockne-type rousing. The minute Pug stepped into that room, where everyone would be sitting around on the benches cold and a little stiff and with a stomach full of butterflies, something would happen to the kids; they would straighten up and their faces would harden, and half ashamed, half awed, they would listen to the few simple and straightforward instructions Pug had for them as if they were listening to the Holy Ghost himself, and then Pug would say, very quietly, very simply, something like, "Good luck, men; we're all counting on you," and they'd fight each other to race out onto the field, shouting and yelling.

Even at the games, Pug said little or nothing directly to the kids. He'd stand at the sideline, chewing through the bit of an empty pipe, sticking his black pinky in it from habit, wearing a brown hat that he wore only for games, a suit, a white shirt, a tie, a brown topcoat. He never took

his eyes off the field; sometimes during a whole game he
would not turn once to look at the bench behind him. He
moved up and down the sidelines to follow the play, his
head deep in his shoulders and pushed forward, his chin
practically on his chest, looking almost like a midget with
all those padded and helmeted giants around, but at the
same time looking without question like the midget in
charge. The student manager stood on his left with his
notebook, Piney Savage on his right. Joe Minotti would
have the bench, Red Warwick would be on the field end of
the phone, Sam Bassey on the press-box end. Minotti
handled the regular substitutions according to a chart
made up by Pug before every game, and when Pug wanted
to pull a certain man or put one in, or send in a play, he'd
have Piney Savage take care of it. Once in a while he'd
send Piney to the bench to tell some kid what he was doing
wrong, and when the players came out it'd be Piney who'd
run over and slap them on the rump and say something
nice. Maybe three, four times a game, Pug would nod to a
man coming out—that's all, just nod, without saying anything, without touching him. But the guy he nodded to
would know that even though there may not have been
ten people in the stands who had noticed what he had
done out there, that Pug had noticed it. It may have been
just a good solid block at the right time, a cross block
when a cross block had been needed but when the guy
was out of position for it and really had to scramble to
make it, and had scrambled, and had made it, and it may
not even have been worth anything in the long run because
maybe the play flopped anyhow, but at least the kid
would know, and the other kids would know, that Pug was
watching, and that when they really came through, Pug
saw it.

Sure, Pug was cold. He was cold, he was tough, he was
hard, sometimes almost vicious. It wasn't just that he

wanted to win; he had to win. There wasn't much point
worrying about what you did, because when you won everything was great, and when you lost everything was wrong,
and the Townbirds crucified you. Sure, he had Phil Lichey
shoot dope into kids whose knees hurt, or whose ankles or
elbows were sore and bandaged. The shots made the pain
go away and the kids played hard. So what if a kid could
get hurt that way—a kid could get hurt a lot of ways. Football's a rough game, and no one plays it very long without
getting hurt once in a while. It wasn't Pug's job to worry
about that. It was his job to win, and if their knees were
too sensitive to play on, he'd have Phil Lichey fix it so
their knees felt fine and they could play hard, and then
maybe we'd win. Two years before, in Pug's first year, he
had a fair halfback who was also, incidentally, the star
dash and broadjump man on the track team, who was
a far better and more valuable track man than he was a
halfback. The guy wrenched his knee in a game and sat
out practice all week, but then Pug doped him up before
the next game and the kid played. When the track coach
heard about it, he went on the rampage, but it didn't do any
good. Track doesn't rate; football does. If the football
coach has to chance ruining a great track man forever in
order to have a mediocre halfback ready for one game, he
just goes ahead and does it.

I walked along the edge of the field and looked over
the boys. They weren't doing much, just signal drill and
pass protection and things like that. I spotted Dancer; Piney
had him working on the halfback option, where he ran
right and could either pass or run. But it was just dummy
work, with no blocking or tackling. Yesterday's scrimmage
had been the last big push before the game, and tomorrow
would be even lighter. Pug had really worked the boys into
condition, and now was just easing them into the game.

There were a few scattered people around watching, the

gray football buffs in scarves and overcoats, some of whom never missed a practice from year to year. I saw Andy Rivers across the field, talking to a couple of guys, and waved vigorously to show him I was on the job. Then I took out some paper and hunkered down at the edge of the field and watched everything very closely and pretended to be writing things down.

I always got itchy watching the guys work out. Looking at them prancing around out there, I'd begin to hate them for being able to prance around in a way that, hard as I tried, was always beyond me. In a lot of ways I agree with old Irvine: football is a pretty silly game, especially when you think of all those drunken old grads waving pennants, or a bunch like the Birds, yet there's something about seeing big sweaty guys—and especially the Negroes, with their faces and arms glistening and shiny—running around and throwing the ball and charging into each other that is more than I can resist. A lot of it, I guess, is just the feel of physical contact, which is great when you're all warmed up and loose. To cut down someone with a nice block or a hard tackle and feel the two bodies, yours and his, crunching together and smashing into the hard ground, to feel the smart slap of the pads against your shoulders and your legs, to smell the grass even as you go down, as you hit and slide—there's something primally satisfying in this, something strong and climactic. Those are the sweetest bruises a man ever knows, and nothing ever hurts that good again. I have a theory about nervous women; they miss this sort of thing, this steam-valve release, and that's what causes half their migraines and frigidity and nagging. But that's beside the point, and the point is that it bothers me to watch other guys doing something very well that I probably love a lot more than they do, but can't do half as well. And not only do I love the game more, but I have enough brains and sensitivity to be aware of the great satisfactions of this love. Dancer, for instance, used to feel exactly the same way before he came to college, and one time I asked him why he used to like football, what it did for him, and he thought a long time with that intelligent face of his and then he kind of shrugged and said, "It feels good."

I loved football so much I even used to play sand-lot football, and in the Bronx, where you had to search between the rocks to find the sand—the big rocks, because the small ones were hidden under the weeds and the crab grass and the dandelions. The el was practically right over us, and we had to stop when a train went by because we couldn't hear the signals. The field we played on was almost triangular, so that for half the game the sidelines closed in on you as you moved toward your goal line. We were all in junior high, and nobody had much money, and I don't think we had two complete uniforms among the eleven of us. There'd be a helmet here and a pair of trousers or shoulder pads there, and sometimes a jersey from the five-and-ten, but that was about it. I played in dungarees and a sweatshirt until I was twelve or thirteen, when I traded a kid a couple of big rats I caught in the marshes around Bruckner Boulevard for his old helmet. He traded because it was spring, and football season was far away, but his mother wouldn't let him in with the rats, and the next day he wanted his helmet back. I wouldn't give it—if I had had a bike or a baseball glove or anything else to trade, I would have given him that instead, but I wasn't going to give back the helmet. All summer I rubbed oil and saddle soap into it, and the following fall I felt like Sammy Baugh out there, and I didn't even think of the ruts or the rocks any more—as if the helmet were a Shield of Virtue or something, a magic amulet, and nothing could hurt me then. That helmet had a smell I can still smell. Even when I just think of the smell it brings everything else back, including the faces of some of the kids we played against. We called ourselves the Crotona Crusaders, because we all lived near Crotona Park, and I was captain and played quarterback and called the plays, because I was the smartest and knew the most about football, and since we didn't have a coach I really ran things. We had a pretty good team, beat a lot of older teams. I spent a lot of time working up plays and formations, with diagrams and all, most of which I got out of books from the East Tremont Branch Library. This was before the T-formation was used everywhere, and once I got a book by Clark Shaughnessy, and that year I guess we were the only T-formation sand-lot team in the country. I never again enjoyed football as much as I did then. I was pretty heady from my success among the rocks and the crab grass, and I went out for quarterback at DeWitt Clinton, confident I'd make it. But the coach wanted to carry only three quarterbacks, and I was fourth among four, so I shifted to the line to stay on the squad. I had to shift down again to meet the college competition, and since I was already at the bottom notch, I shifted myself right off the team.

Practice ended and I followed the guys down the run-way to the locker room. Football players aren't only bigger than other people; they run heavier. They really do. They sounded like a buffalo charge, especially down there where everything echoes along the concrete halls. I checked first to see if anyone was hurt. Kinney was in the whirlpool, but he always was. He was about nineteenth string, and used up more tape and bandages and got more rubdowns and whirlpool baths than the rest of the team put together. The other guys were showering, or going to the showers, or coming out, leaving big wet footprints on the cement or on the scale, or else getting dressed at their lockers. Everything was damp and steamy. There was a lot of noise. The boys are usually worked up after practice, and they were all shouting and laughing and kidding each other. Most football players are quiet when they're out on their own, but together they're pretty rowdy.

I walked around a bit and kidded along with the guys, and asked them about practice and everything, as if I was looking for stuff for my story. But I really just got a kick out of joking with them. Once in a while I'd feel sheepish doing it, and get an uncomfortable flash of myself talking with them, talking like them. It was one of the things about myself I least appreciated. I'd tell myself they ought to be scrounging around trying to talk to me, but I knew they didn't give a damn if they talked to me or not. Whenever there's a crowd of eight or ten people at a party, and one person is holding the floor and seems to be performing for the whole crowd, he's really not. He's putting on his show for maybe one person in that crowd, and if that person goes to the bathroom or something, suddenly the guy stops performing, everybody stops, and they just keep up polite conversation until he gets back and they can start in again. Well, I'm the type no one ever performs for. When I go to the bathroom, everyone keeps right on the way they were. They don't even notice I'm gone. I could drop dead in the bathroom and no one'd even know it until the next person had to go.

Anyhow, I was ribbing Janowski about getting fat, slapping him on the stomach and everything, when all of a sudden the place went dead quiet. Willie Plasby had walked in and was climbing onto a chair at the end of the aisle between the lockers. Willie Plasby was yell chief, which meant he handled the big white megaphone at the games and led the cheers. (*All right now, everybody—the Locomotive! The Locomotive! Let's go!*) He was an enthusiastic kid, with red hair and freckles, and I'm sure he slept in his honorary "U" sweater.

Willie raised his hand for silence from the chair, even

though everyone was already pretty quiet. Most of the guys went on dressing, sort of half turned the other way.

"Fellas," Willie began. "Fellas . . ." He squinted when he spoke. "I want to invite all of you personally, and remind you all of the big pregame rally and bonfire tomorrow night in front of the econ building. We're gonna have the biggest rally ever, and want to send you fellas off to the best season we Eagles have ever had."

Chuck Janowski lifted his leg and farted. The rest of the guys cheered. Except Dancer, who just sat on the bench in front of his locker and ignored everything, looking like the only intelligent guy around.

Willie laughed and shrugged, blushing a little. "That's all right, fellas . . . We know how important school spirit is to you fellas out there on the field, and believe me, we're all working our darndest to get everybody out there Saturday cheering their heads off and backing you to the hilt. We're gonna have the biggest and best card and booster section in history, and we've got some really great new yells we've been practicing. You'll hear them all at the rally tomorrow night, and we're gonna have Coach Walters introduce each and every one of you individually to the crowd. So don't forget to be there—the bonfire starts at sundown, and the rally starts right afterward. You can all assemble in a group behind the stand we'll set up; Coach Walters will be there to lead you onstage. Do you have any questions, fellas?"

No one had any questions. The invitation from Willie was a formality: a notice on the bulletin board from Pug had already informed the squad that their presence would be required.

"One more thing—" Willie waved a sheet of paper. "We're gonna paste one of these over every toilet bowl in the school, and we can start right in here. And we even have a volunteer squad of boosters on their way at this very moment to the Tech campus—to paste them up over *their* toilets, too! Look, fellas!" Willie held the paper up with both freckled hands.

PLEASE FLUSH
Tech Needs Water

"What'd'ya think of that, fellas?"

"You better be careful, Willie," Chuck Janowski shouted, "bending over all them toilet bowls . . ."

Willie laughed a little, then waved and got down from the chair. "See you all at the big rally," he called, squinting, smiling. He looked around at the fellows uneasily, then left.

On the way out, I dropped in on Pug and found Willie with him. Pug sat biting his pipe, his feet on the desk. Pug had the smallest, narrowest feet I ever saw on a man.

"Hey, we're gonna have a big story for you at the rally," Willie said. "We're gonna have Pug and Dancer present the little kid that got hurt the other day with a "U" sweater. You can take pictures and everything."

"We already got a picture of him getting a football," I said. "What are we gonna do next, give him a scholarship? He didn't even get hurt."

"Well, it wasn't my idea."

"Andy's?"

"Yes, if you must know," Willie admitted. "Mr. Rivers suggested it, and I said I thought it was a very good idea."

"It's a great idea," I said. "I was just kidding you."

"No, you weren't. You meant it. But anyway, we're working very hard on it. We got a couple of girls downtown buying a sweater that'll fit, and then they're going to have to dye it red and sew the "U" on and everything. I told

Mr. Rivers it would be a lot of trouble, but he said it'd be worth it, it'd get us a lot of publicity and everything."

"Have you spoken to the kid's mother?"

"I spoke to his father. He said it was a fine idea."

"Then we all agree," I said.

"I've got some work to do, Willie," Pug said. "See you at the rally."

"Sure thing, Coach. I realize how busy you must be." Willie bowed and backed out the door.

"Any news for the press?" I asked.

"I predict we'll win by twelve touchdowns."

"Is anyone hurt or anything?"

"I don't know. Ask Lichey."

"Will you give us a starting lineup tomorrow?"

"I suppose so."

"Any surprises?"

"I haven't given it any thought yet."

"I'll bet. But all right—I'll let you go to work."

"I never work. I'm going to the movies tonight."

"Oh—did you get those Tech movies?"

"Yeah. We traded each other four games."

"Four? You'll be watching all night."

"I suspect so. How you doing with Dan?"

"Fine. I don't see what everybody's so concerned about. I'll drop over tonight and do a little preliminary work— brush up on nouns and verbs and things like that."

"Don't keep him up too late. He looked sleepy today— said he was up studying with you last night."

"I'll have him in bed by nine."

"Okay. And help him work out a decent program this term, will you? He had too many tough courses last year."

"He's very ambitious."

"So am I."

"And so am I," I said.

"You saw Benny?"

"Yes."

"He paid you?"

"Yes."

"Well, you're not earning it here."

"I was just leaving. Here, have a pack of Lords."

CHAPTER NINE

Outside, I saw Andy Rivers down the block, talking to someone on the sidewalk, standing in the late afternoon shadow of the gym but still wiping his forehead. In fact, it was the white handkerchief that caught my eye. I yelled, but he didn't hear me. He shook hands with the guy after shifting the handkerchief to his left hand and bent over to get in his car. I yelled again, but he was already inside. I ran, waving the stories, shouting. The car was parked tight and Andy, who was the world's worst driver because he didn't have any co-ordination or anything, had trouble getting out. He was just swinging clear when I came up shouting and waving the paper. He finally heard me and stopped, the nose of the car stuck out in the street. He looked as if I had, out of pure malice, caused him some monumental inconvenience. I leaned in the open window and reached across the seat and handed him the stories. He was puffing enough for him to have been the one who just ran a whole block.

"The practice story—will you take it down and save me a trip—got the Townbird stuff here, too."

Andy looked at them—looked at the paper, really, because they were folded and he didn't open them, and then tossed them onto the seat.

"Much appreciated," I said.

"Remember this when you turn in your carfare voucher. Did the runt see you about tomorrow night?"

"Yes. I'll get some pictures and everything."

"Try to get a coupla good ones this time." He nodded and I pulled my head out and he drove off, the white handkerchief still in his left hand, his left hand on the wheel, the handkerchief unfurling like a white standard, like the raccoon tails the hotshots tag on their motorcycles.

It was pretty unbearable going across campus. They were all over. For every upperclassman there seemed to be twenty freshmen, the boys in red beanies, the girls in mismatched socks, one red, one white, and with red ribbons in their hair. Every year they look younger, and this year they looked about thirteen. I couldn't even bring myself to examine the girls very closely. Above the left side of the entrance to the Union, next to the huge and gloriously ugly bas-relief in sandstone showing the state's history and greatness, with heroic figures of plowing farmers and smoking trains, with herds of cattle and city buildings, a big WEL-COME! sign hung permanently. Every few days they'd change the sign over the right half: FUTURE FARMERS OF AMERICA, GIRLS STATE, INDUSTRY AND PROGRESS ASSOCIATION, CONGRESS OF CONSERVATION AND RESOURCE USAGE; and now they had up the funniest and saddest sign of all, in great red capitals: FRESHMEN.

Welcome, indeed. Welcome to the great halls and crowded empty classrooms, little boys, little girls. Welcome to our pleasant green-grassed Nirvana where everyone knows what Soc 2 is and worries about Hum 14, but no one knows the name of the Secretary of State or ever heard of Pakistan. Welcome especially, you who come determined not to learn anything, anything at all, to get through four years absolutely unchanged, just the way you came, who consider any attempt upon anyone's part to teach you any-

thing as an insult, a dirty punch below-the-belt, for of all
the thousands who come here to vegetate in our little intellectual hothouse, you alone carry the inevitable germ of success within you. You come as paragons, as whole and perfect examples of what our great country can best produce
the most of, sans wit, grace, charm, humor, brains, sans
even curiosity, sans even the ability to fail in your ambition.

You will find much here to satisfy you, little boys and
girls: formal dances, informal dances, wienie roasts, dates
before and after football and basketball games, cokes full
of shaved ice in the Union, petting on the front porches
of sororities and dorms and lying on the back seats of
convertibles and sedans. You will undoubtedly take further,
although more restrained pleasure, in watching white
Buicks driving slowly through campus on class breaks with
paper signs on both sides saying SHEILA FOR HOMECOMING
QUEEN. And especially for the boys we have beer busts and
drag races through town, during which you can play
chicken with the guys in the other cars and throw empty
bottles out the window, intramural touch-football, ROTC,
paddling—after you become an active yourself—of fraternity pledges, and several thousand assorted libidinous fe-
males. For the girls we have, for instance, bells that clang
when the toilet paper is touched in the girls' washroom at
fraternity parties. We also have the dean of women's annual
welcoming speech in which, through great effort of will,
and because she feels the hotly moral breaths of your
parents on her neck, she will sing you the praises of con-
nubial bliss, the blissfulness of which, she will warn, becomes when de-connubialized such pure horror as to make
her grow pale and sore of heart, although deep down the
good Dean knows, as you and I, that acne and overeating
have caused more sadness than fornication. And knows too,
that it all avails nothing, for if you have not already, you
soon will lose your precious flower, your noble rose, your

petaled and unbroken valve, as if by destiny, and probably to some pimpled Aggie major, the great prize after
such long cherishment going literally as a pearl to some
swineherd, all a waste, all irony, without even glory, without even the romance of Evil, of rapacity or lust—but given
sloppily after three whiskey sours in the bushes behind
some parking lot to a fumbling and moist-eyed boy studying watershed management and animal husbandry. And
you will not even feel bad, for you will soon learn you are
only a friend among friends, and that in many ways you
are quite justified in thinking of yourself as a still unde-
filed flower of virtue and morality, for at least you still
pick and choose to some extent, and your sin seems as nothing when you meet the little girl everybody calls Score-
card because she's had so many football players on her,
and the girl who people quite accurately insist would
lay on the top of a tree, and the fellow whose black book
includes the dates of his girls' menstrual cycles, and finally the considerable number of girls who leave quietly in
the middle of semesters, new initiates into the not-always-
secret Society of the Sisters of Ste. Enceinte, for which
all coeds are frighteningly and forever eligible.

Welcome all, boys and girls, to our little state-supported
orgiastic department store, where everything has been carefully arranged to be most pleasing to you, and least disturbing, where you can make contacts and become well-
rounded and where after four years you may, with your
parents beaming at each black-robed arm, march forth in
your cap and gown, no longer worried about Soc 2 or Hum
14, and still not knowing the name of the Secretary of
State or quite where, exactly, Pakistan is, or why anyone
should even care.

Mr. Manquero, my old English teacher, was always
bitching about the football players, but what he could
never quite understand was that nobody brought those guys

here to *learn* anything in the first place, that nobody even mentioned classes or exams when they not only gave them a free ride, but begged them to take it. Besides, going to class when you're playing football, when you're on the field two or three hours a day for six days a week, when you're eating all the right foods and getting ten hours of sleep a night and when every muscle in your body is trim and hard and flexible, when your mind is filled with a hundred plays and formations and positions and stances— going to class then is about as satisfying as coitus interruptus. If you want students, you should hire students. When you hire football players, you get football players. At least nobody's misled when it comes to the hundred or so guys brought here every year as athletes. Sure, the jockstraps don't belong in any place that pretends to be concerned about education, but Christ, how many of the other twelve thousand students do? Manquero said that in the old days a really educated man had to be self-educated, because unless he happened to be rich he couldn't get past high school. But then we opened up colleges to everyone and in the process they got so stinking bad that now we're right back where we started. Of course, he pretty much blamed all this on football, which I think is a little overstated. It wasn't just football. College football isn't any phonier than anything else, in college or out.

Things were even worse at the House. Everyone had arrived and we had our first suit-and-tie dinner, with Giffling in his glory ringing his water glass with a fork and saying grace and welcoming everyone back and all of us singing the fraternity song. But at least the cook was back, too, and the food was good. I talked as much as necessary to the idiots alongside me to get through the meal—saying things like, "Sure I remember that time Danny got crocked last year and puked all over Bob Weister's bed. Yeah, wasn't

that something? Great. We sure had some great times."
And then we had another prayer and a few more fraternal
songs after dessert and then were supposed to, as Giffling
suggested, renew old ties of friendship in the living room or
the game room until eight-thirty, when we would have our
first House meeting of the year, to discuss a number of extremely important matters.

"Gotta go to the bathroom," I mumbled and started
moving, as inconspicuously as possible, against the tide.
Christ, it was noisy. Everyone was yattering away at the
same time, and they all sounded like great prospects for
the Birds. Which of course they were. Anyhow, I waited
in the bathroom until the coast was clear and then sneaked
upstairs. Giffling would probably miss me in a few minutes;
he looked upon me as his hundredth sheep.

I got on the hall phone upstairs and dialed Pug's house.
A couple of guys were still wandering about, but I looked
very businesslike and ignored them. Caroline answered.

"Hello, Mrs. Walters, this is Jack Wyant, reporter for
the Midland *Standard.* I wanted to get in touch with Coach
Walters, but I heard he was going to be spending the
evening watching films of Tech's games tonight. Do you
know if that's true?"

"Yes," Caroline said. "He doesn't expect to be back until
midnight."

"I see. Do you think he'll be down there watching in,
say, a half hour from now?"

"Yes. I'm sure he will."

"Thank you very much, Mrs. Walters. Good-by."

"Good-by."

When I hung up, one of the guys going by said, "Meeting's gonna start right away."

"You go ahead," I said. "I'm on my way."

I dialed Peggy's number and got her mother.

"Hello. This is Dr. Egbert, history department. May I

speak to your daughter Peggy—her registration creden-
tials for my course have become misplaced and I—"

"One minute."

Peggy came and said, "Hello, who is this?"

"Dr. Egbert, known as Jack to his friends."

"Hello!"

"Not so enthusiastic. Look, I'm tied up at the House
tonight—first meeting and everything, all very rah-rah. What
about tomorrow night? I gotta cover the rally, but then we'll
be free."

"Okay."

"I'll meet you in front of the chem building."

"Be happy to, Dr. Egbert."

I undressed in my room and got into my robe and went
down the hall and shaved and took a quick shower. No one
was around. I returned, dressed, and hurried down the
back stairway, then across the dark yard and through the
juniper hedges.

My first stop was Ape Hall, where I found Dan lying on
his bunk reading a book. *Huckleberry Finn.*

"You like it?" I asked.

He was stretched out with his head resting on his hand,
his elbow on the bed. He shrugged. "It's kinda funny, I
guess. It's not written very smooth though. The writing itself, I mean."

"What are you reading it for?"

"They use it in this course."

"What course?"

"American lit. I'm gonna take it."

"Don't be crazy. It's a tough course. You don't need it."

"I should read more."

"I bet I know who said that. Anyhow, we'll discuss it
later. Pug said you looked tired today—maybe you should
go to bed early tonight."

"I wasn't tired."

"You looked tired."

"I was bored."

"They ain't sending you through school and giving you a priceless education and everything to look bored out there—you know that, don't you? What are you doing now, sitting around waiting for your girl friend to get finished down at the five-and-dime?"

"Why don't you like her?"

"I like her fine."

"What were you doing this morning, checking up on me?"

"Cut it, will you? I was downtown and going right by the Y and everything, so I just said hello. Is she coming to the rally tomorrow?"

"Why?"

"Because I got a date with Peggy and I thought we could all get together after."

"All right."

"Good. I'd just like to get to know her, that's all. Any friend of yours is a friend of mine. I gotta go now. Stay home, why don't you, and get some sleep tonight."

"Sure. You be the boss. I'll do whatever you say."

"I'm just trying to help you, for your own good."

I walked to the gym. The campus was dark and I couldn't see the students' faces or anything very well, so it wasn't too bad. The gym was locked up every night and only the coaches and the people who worked there had keys. I went around back and climbed on top of the wooden outdoor storage shed, grabbed the metal grating over the first-floor window and climbed up it until I could reach the second floor men's-room window, which was open a couple of inches. I shoved it up some more and boosted myself up and in. Then I went down the hall to the empty and dark basketball stands, down through them and down the ramp toward exit 5, quietly, and along the hall to the projection room. It was dark in there, too, naturally, with the door closed and no light under it. I waited outside a few minutes and then heard Pug's voice, tired, strained, sleepy: "Play that one over, Red. I think the end was out again."

I backed up slowly in the darkness and went up the ramp and through the stands and out a regular door; they were only locked from the outside. It was a quarter to nine. Pug was probably exhausted. He worked harder than anyone on campus, but if he had four games to watch tonight, he'd stay and watch them. Sometimes I felt sorry for Pug, knocking himself out all the time for the goddamn team.

I walked up Magnolia five blocks and along Quincy for two blocks and knocked on the door. Caroline let me in and closed the door behind me.

"Hello," I said.

She just looked at me but didn't say anything, her black eyes moving uneasily, uncertainly, the way some people's hands are always moving. I went on into the living room and she followed. I sat down on the couch. She remained standing while I looked up at her. White blouse, gray skirt, leather sandals. Nice legs.

"Let me make you one," she said.

"Okay." I didn't like to drink, but Caroline always got sore when I turned one down.

She went into the kitchen and brought me a gin and tonic.

"Thanks." I raised the glass to her, but she didn't move or go for her glass. I drank some. She sure made a stiff drink. "It's been a while," I said.

She nodded, then took her glass and sat down, not on the couch, but in the big armchair on the other side of the coffee table in front of me. She crossed her legs, holding the half-empty glass in her lap. Then she drank the rest of it, stood up, and went into the kitchen. She came back with a new drink and returned to the chair, crossing her legs.

I just looked at her for a while without saying anything. She acted like this sometimes until she had a few drinks, and I didn't mind waiting, looking. Caroline was the only woman I ever had who really excited me—I mean just looking at her, just seeing her getting in or out of a car, or bending over putting away groceries in the kitchen. Except maybe the first one, who was a sixteen-year-old New York Jewess. She worked one summer as a playground supervisor in Crotona Park. I was fourteen then, and first noticed her sitting at a wooden table filling out some report forms. I watched her from another bench, staring at her thighs through the chicken wire of an empty trash basket which was directly between us. It made an impressive image, and it has remained with me. She had black hair, which looked very good along with her white uniform, and disturbingly prominent breasts. I got to know her by telling her I was looking for my sixteen-year-old younger brother. We chatted gaily for a bit, and then I admitted I had really been stopped by the view she presented in her shorts.

"Those are very pretty pick panties you're wearing," I remarked, in what at the time I considered the ultimate in seductive conversation.

She blushed and was about to get angry before she remembered: "White," she corrected.

"Oh, well. Think how unnerved you'd have been if I guessed right."

"I wouldn't have been unnerved," she said.

She was a very broad-minded talker—and boy, we had some great talks; after all, I was fourteen, I had a lot to learn—but otherwise she was pretty cautious, and it took me most of the summer to make out with her. Our first time was one night in the bushes on the hill overlooking the playground where she worked, right where my father strolled every day spearing Popsicle wrappers and pulling them off the point with his fingers, sliding them into the big burlap bag hung around his shoulder. I had her the rest of that summer, and used to hang around during the day hungrily watching her in her white shorts looking after the ping-pong balls and the shuffleboard equipment and um- piring volleyball games between the kids. But since then none of them really excited me much outside of bed except Caroline. And of all of them I guess Caroline was the only one who was really beautiful, although Marie Wu, the Chinese girl, came close. But Caroline had everything, beautiful hair, perfect features, a marvelous pair of breasts, long thin legs—and those uneasy, guilty eyes, which gave everything the final touch it needed.

From the beginning it was luck, an accident, and because of that unlike any of the others, all of whom I had to plan and work for. Last year I had to see Pug about something and Red Warwick said he had gone home to get ready to go upstate somewhere for a talk to an alumni group. I hurried over to catch him, but he had already left. Caroline came to the door, in her robe, a glass in her hand. I found out afterward they had just had a fight before he had left. That was why she was drinking, she said. They were always having fights then, although I didn't know that. This year they had stopped fighting; they just let each other alone, never even touched each other, hardly even talked. But I didn't know any of this at that time. I didn't even know her, although I had seen her around a few times. But I never thought much about her or noticed her particularly; she was Pug's wife and there didn't seem any more point think- ing about her than about a picture of a girl on a billboard. I didn't do anything that first time, although I guess I could have. All I could think of was Pug, or at least—as I watched her sitting there in her robe with her legs crossed and her eyes darting—of what Pug would think if he knew I was sitting there and she was sitting there. She talked a lot that night, more than she ever did since, but even what she said didn't help. I don't know if I didn't believe what she was saying, or if I just didn't believe I was really sitting there watching her legs and hearing what she was saying. And I would never have gone back, except that she called me about a week later, at the House. She asked me if I was Jack Wyant, reporter for the Midland *Standard,* and said that she was Mrs. Walters, and that I could have a very interesting story about Pug taking a trip to see some high school coach if I dropped over that night at nine o'clock.

She was twenty-nine then. "How old are you?" she asked that night.

"Twenty-eight," I said. "I was in the Marines a while and then worked around for a few years."

I was afraid I would have trouble facing Pug after that, because I really liked the guy, but I didn't. Not at all. Sure, I was getting something behind his back, but I wouldn't have been, wouldn't have even tried, if he hadn't turned his back on it in the first place, practically inviting someone to come and get it. If not me, someone else, so why not me? Besides, the husband Caroline was always complaining about never seemed to be the same person I saw standing with his binoculars on top of the ten-foot wooden stand in the middle of the practice field, or sitting in his office in the catacombs, under the pictures of his former teams, stuffing his pinky into his pipe, with his small, almost delicate feet on the desk. So I didn't have any trouble at all talking to him. In fact, we got along fine. He was a good coach and a good guy; he treated me all right and I had no complaints. In a way, we were pretty good friends, and he'd even bitch to me sometimes about Benny or Andy Rivers, or even about Irvine, because he felt comfortable with me. I guess you could go so far as to say he trusted me.

I saw Caroline whenever I got a chance. Sometimes it

was once a week, sometimes a couple of times a month, sometimes two or three nights in a row. We always stayed in the house, never went out where people could see us. It was best off season, when Pug traveled a lot giving talks and making contacts, recruiting players, attending meetings. Most people think football coaches work only a couple of months a year, during the season, but they work twelve months a year, three hundred and sixty-five days. For the life of me I wouldn't want Irvine's job or Andy's, but of all the jobs I know of, the one I'd want least would be Pug's —especially if I had a wife like Caroline. Pug lived on pills. At first when Caroline started telling me about him, I thought right away he was queer. He wouldn't be the first football player, or football coach, either. But he wasn't queer, he was sick. That's when I learned about the pills, and about his stomach, and about the headaches. He took pills all the time, all kinds of pills, but did it pretty carefully and no one knew about it except Caroline—and me, because she told me. Only the pills didn't do any good, and he still couldn't sleep, and his stomach was so bad he could hardly eat anything, and his head always hurt. It was kind of funny in a way that a guy who had the guts and the drive to play first-string guard at 145 pounds for three years at Minnesota now had to live on pills—and that even they didn't really help.

"He's watching the films," I said. "I checked to make sure."

"He'll probably watch them all night. He'll watch them all twice to make sure he doesn't miss anything."

We were quiet again for a few minutes, and then I said, "Anyhow, we've got a few hours. Maybe we shouldn't wait too long, though."

She shrugged. "I . . . I just feel like talking . . . I don't know."

She picked that up from Pug. He was always saying
I don't know.

"Just talking?" I said. "Just?"

"Yes," she said. "I'm sorry . . . I just wanted to talk to
somebody. I didn't think you'd mind."

"We're both taking a lot of chances just for a chat."

"You say that because you have people to talk to all the
time. You've got your girl friends. How many do you have
now—ten? twenty?"

"What do you want to talk about? Maybe we can talk
for a while and then—"

"No. Just talk."

"All right," I said. I had my clue, and saw what I had
to do. "What do you want to talk about—art? literature?
politics?"

"Please, Jack."

"I'm trying to be accommodating."

She was quiet for a moment. She finished her drink.

"You haven't any feelings," she said. "You're the only
person I've ever known who doesn't have anything—any
feelings—any ideals—not even stupid ones—"

"Of course not. Who said I did? Who does?"

"Pug does."

"Then why don't you talk to him? I've been around
here too much for you to start telling me about Pug's
ideals. Tell Andy, it'd make a good column. Young Coach
So Idealistic He Won't—"

"All right," she said.

"That's me." I said. "Cold as an ice cube. And without
a single goddamn ideal." I put my glass down and went
over to her chair. She stiffened and watched me coming.
"Only I'm willing to do what Pug won't do."

"That's all you want to do."

"It's one of the things I want to do. And that you want
to do too—only you feel better talking about ideals first.

Why don't we talk about ideals after? Then if Pug comes back he'll feel more at home, finding us talking about something he's familiar with instead of doing something that he's so unfamiliar with he may not even know what it is."

I was over her now, sitting on the arm of the chair, my hands on her, coming down over her—her eyes finally still, frozen—like I was coming down for a drink of water over one of those fountains in Crotona Park.

I left around ten-thirty, feeling good. I really enjoyed Caroline. At first, things had not worked out well for us last year, because I used to sit around and wait until she was ready, or until I thought she was ready, which usually took her around three drinks. One night she didn't seem to ever want to get ready, and I was impatient and got sore at her and called her a few names. It worked sensationally, and I finally caught on. She was sore at Pug not simply because he wouldn't give her what she wanted, but because even when he gave it, when he used to give it, he wouldn't make any effort to get it. From then on she'd either be on top of me the minute I walked in, or would have to be dragged upstairs. And it was always better when I had to drag her, especially if I got sore first and insulted her a little. It helps sometimes to get sore at girls and tell them off. A lot of them like being berated.

I walked across the dark campus, past all the lighted dorms where the girls were discussing religion and sex and freshman English, and went in Ape Hall. Dan's door was locked. I knew he might be asleep in there, but was pretty sure he wasn't. I used the duplicate I had made from his key when I borrowed it last year. The room was empty. I went back to the House.

The meeting was over, and from the sidewalk outside I could see everyone in the living room renewing old friendships. I went around through the hedges and the parking lot and up the back stairway to my room. A piece of paper was tacked to my door: "Andy Rivers keeps calling—important." I tore the paper off and dialed the *Standard* office on the hall phone. One of the guys came up the stairs.

"Hey, Jack—you missed the meeting and everything."

"I'm very busy right now," I said.

I got Andy on the phone and he told me that the little kid Dan bowled over had died.

"A concussion or something. Who knows? He just dropped dead, just like that. I'm glad you found enough time from your busy schedule to call in. Go over to the hospital and find out what happened."

"Giffling wants to see you," the guy said when I hung up. He had been standing there in the hall waiting for me to finish.

"Christ," I said. "Will you guys leave me alone? Go down and shake hands with somebody or something." I turned and hurried down the back stairs so I wouldn't have to meet anybody.

CHAPTER TEN

The hospital was west, right on the edge of town, in what had been a scrub meadow a few years back but which had since given way to faceless tracts of square, brightly colored houses, now crowded against the high wire gate on all sides. As we reached the top of Wayne Hill above the old meadow, along what was Pinckney Street in town but became U.S. 43 outside, the houses below us seemed like pieces from a Monopoly set, and the white hospital with its right-angled wings looked in the moonlight like a white swastika with a leg chopped off.

The truck driver double-clutched as we inched over the crest. He drove a Mack flatbed, with a cab smelling of leather and diesel fuel, and carried crated washing machines, coming out of Chicago and heading south. The driver was a thin dark guy with a thin mustache and a narrow face.

"I wouldn't normally have picked chup," he said. "We ain't supposed to."

"I appreciate it," I said. "That's it up ahead."

"I know." He tapped his air brake lightly, and the *choot! choot!* sounded loud in the cab. The truck bucked each time he touched the brake. He shifted down and rolled slowly toward the hospital entrance. "I sure hope your mother's all right," he said.

"I'm sure she will be."

"Ain't it the way, though—car breaking down at a time like that."

"Yes," I said. I swung open the heavy door and hopped out while he was still rolling and slammed the door shut. He waved and picked up speed again with a roar at my ear level.

I showed the woman at the desk my press card. "Rending," I said. "Timmy Rending—the kid who was hurt yesterday and—"

"Oh, yes."

"Could I see the doctor for a minute?"

"If he's free. Have a seat."

I sat on a smooth, polished wooden bench with a curved seat and a curved back. There were a few other benches and some tables with magazines. Only two other people were in the waiting room, an old couple sitting together watching me. I read the copper plaque on the wall, commemorating the erection of the new hospital building in 1954. Listed as chairman of the fund-raising committee was Benjamin K. Johnson. Just like Benny to get in on something like that—something noble and wholesome, so that when you tried to tell somebody what a slob he was, they'd start in about him being president of this and chairman of that and active in something else, and then they'd say, "What'd you ever do for your community?" When Benny ran for Congress that time, he used to run ads in the paper every day with a foot-long list of his civic activities. The guy he ran against was a young lawyer, a graduate of Harvard Law School, who knew a hell of a lot about taxation and urban development and farm problems and quite a few other things. Naturally he was opposed by the *Standard* and every responsible civic and business leader

in the community, all of whom enthusiastically supported
Benny. After all, Benny belonged to the Kiwanis and used
to play football at the U and was in the Marines in World
War II. But as it turned out, the hick farmers didn't give
a damn what the *Standard* said, and the niggers in their
shacks were too ignorant even to know what it said, or
what the Kiwanis was, and the unions were too insolent
to pay attention to their betters, and somehow Benny got
beat. Whenever I'm ready to completely lose faith in this
country, I always remind myself that Benny lost. He lost,
I tell myself, and then I feel better. I guess it must be a
little of my father's blood still in me.

After a few minutes a young doctor, probably an interne,
came over. He wore a white jacket tied back with strings.
I got up and we shook hands.

"Dr. Mansfield."

"Jack Wyant from the *Standard*. You be kind enough to
give me some information about the Rending boy?" I took
out some folded-over copy paper and a stub pencil. My
memory was good and I never really had to write things
down, but people didn't like talking to you if you weren't
writing something down.

"Yes. Concussion. Cortical occlusion. Hemorrhaging."

"What time was he brought in?"

"The receptionist has that."

"Was he conscious?"

"Dead on arrival."

"Did he die on the way?"

"In the ambulance. He was unconscious when they got
to the house. He was unconscious when his father called."

"Did he hurt himself again? Is that why—"

"No. No further injuries. The original concussion did
it."

"Couldn't he have hurt himself again without the parents knowing?"

"Unlikely. It would have to be a terrific blow. This happened when that football player plowed into him yesterday."

"Can you be positive of that?"

"I'm positive," he said.

"I was there when it happened. It didn't seem like much of a bump or anything. The kid even walked away."

"He was out for a while, wasn't he?"

"A minute or so maybe. No more."

"Then he started running and fell down again—"

"I'm not sure," I said. "I don't remember."

"They should have taken him right to a doctor. The coach should have known that. Any blow on the head that causes unconsciousness, even for a second, should be examined by a doctor. Every coach in the country knows that."

"The kid seemed all right. He walked away and—"

"Well, next time you see him, ask him how many football players walked away after bumps on the head last year and died a couple of hours or a couple of days later."

"Do you want me to print what you said about the coach?"

"No. Do you have any other questions?"

"How did he get the blow on the head? Dancer hit him low."

"When he hit the ground, I guess. The blow was on the back of the head. A hard spot in the turf, perhaps. That could do it—if he was knocked high enough and flipped back on his head when he landed."

"Would it have made any difference if he went to a doctor right away?"

"Of course. He would have had a chance then."

"A good chance?"

"Better than he had."

"I see. Are his parents here?"

"Why?"

"I'd like to see them for a moment."

"The mother's in bad shape."

"Maybe I can see the father then."

"Why don't you leave them alone? What do you want— a picture of them crying?"

"I'd like to get a statement."

"I doubt if you'd want to print what you'd get. Now, if there's nothing else I can do for you. . . ?"

"Thank you for your help."

"You're quite welcome."

I got what I needed from the receptionist and called Andy from a phone booth. I gave him everything I had.

"Are his folks there?"

"I've been trying to find them," I said.

"Get me a statement. I'll work this stuff up and wait for it. Hurry up—it's eleven-thirty."

I went back to the woman at the desk. "Are the boy's parents around? I'm really quite a good friend of the family and I'd like to see if I can help in some—"

"They just left. Out toward the parking lot."

I ran out along the cement path and onto the gravel. Coming from the lighted room, I couldn't see much in the lot, even with the moon. A motor started. Two headlights went on across the lot, aimed away from me. I started running over the gravel and tripped in a gully and almost fell. The car turned, and the two glaring white spots blinded me. I put one arm across my face and waved with the other one. The car turned until I was out of the direct beam, and then moved up quietly alongside me, crunching the gravel, and stopped. It was a black Chrysler Imperial. The man driving leaned out and looked up at me. "Yes."

"Sir—I hate to disturb you—are you Mr. Rending?"

He stared up at me without answering, his head stuck out the window, half turned upward, his eyes still, his head

seeming almost a complete thing in itself, detached, inde-
pendent. "What do you want?" he said finally.

"I'm terribly sorry about Timmy . . ."

"Who are you?"

"Jack Wyant—I work for the *Standard*, but I'm also a very
good friend of the fellow who—ran into your son, and—"

"We have nothing to say." He pulled his head in to drive
off, but I put my hands on the window ledge and bent
down. I could see the mother across the seat now. She was
not even looking at me. She stared straight ahead, holding
a handkerchief in her lap.

"I realize what a blow this must be, sir . . . ma'am . . .
I only ask that in your own sadness you be good enough to
think of someone else. I know how hard it must be . . . I
realize what—"

"Let's go." The woman spoke without turning, still staring ahead, as if she were studying something in the light
just past the chrome figure on the hood.

"Stand back," the man said.

"Can't you understand how that poor fellow feels?" I
said. "Can't you imagine what this will do to him? It wasn't
his fault. He's only a kid himself, only eighteen years old,
and now all his life he's going to have this on his conscience. They had to give him something—did you know
that? To calm him down. They got some guys watching
him to make sure he wouldn't do anything to himself. He
broke down and cried when he heard. He broke down and
cried."

"Let's go," the woman said again, without turning, without looking. I don't think she even recognized me from
the other day.

"What do you want us to do?" the man asked.

"Just say a word, that's all—something I can print saying
it's not his fault, that you forgive him, that you don't hold
him responsible. That's all. Just a word. All his life he's go-

ing to have to face this thing and just a word from you can—"

"All right," the man said.

"Don't talk to him," the mother said. "Let's go."

"What do you want to say?" I asked. "Whatever you say will help. Just a word—"

"Print whatever you want," the man said. "Anything you want."

"Let's go," the woman said.

I stepped back. "Thank you," I said. "Thank you."

The motor shuddered and the car jerked forward, throwing gravel, spinning it into the air. The lights stretched across the lot, and then swung toward the entrance and onto the road.

I went inside and called Andy. All he said when I finished was, "Okay." He always acted as if you just fell into everything through luck. He never said *thanks,* never said *good.*

"Are you still going to run that feature on Dan tomorrow?"

"Of course not," he said. His voice sounded even scratchier than normal on the phone.

"Maybe we can use it later," I suggested.

"I threw it away."

"You did?"

"Sure I did. Who the hell wants to read about the goddamn courses he's taking, for Christ's sake? Who reads the sports page to find out about somebody becoming an accountant? What's wrong with you, anyhow?"

"I thought it'd be good background. A lot of people'd be interested."

"Millions. Next time you write about a football player, make a real effort to mention football somewhere, okay? Where is Dan, anyhow? We oughta have something from him."

"He's home sleeping. Why don't you just say he was shocked and everything and sick at heart and how nice the kid was when he went over the other day."

"All right. I'll work something up."

"Don't forget to cut the stuff about the kid out of the rally story."

"I already did. You got any more advice?"

Yeah, I wanted to say. Shove it, shove it. "No," I said.

"All right. See you at practice tomorrow."

I went out to the road and waited. Damn! but it was cold and windy, and nothing seemed to be going by. I was there over an hour and it was miserable, my teeth chattering, my toes numb, my eyes watering. That goddamn icy black wind had nothing to do but blow every last bit of human warmth out through my clothes. I was shivering, and began to feel sorry for myself, something I usually try to avoid. And waiting out there in the dark, in that cold, staring across at the hospital, I began to think of the kid too. I hadn't had time earlier; I had been too busy. But out there I had trouble not thinking of him. Boy, I thought, he's really cold. Poor goddamn little stupid kid. Christ, kid, I thought—that's what happens when you get in the way. You got to stay out of the way. You got to learn. I found myself talking to myself like that, giving the kid a lecture on how to get along in life, something he really had no desperate need of any more. The whole thing was pretty gruesome. I felt lousy—the cold, the kid, everything. I kicked at pebbles to warm up and work off some of the crummy feeling, but I was so cold it hurt my toes. For God's sake, I hadn't wanted to get into anything like this. But what the hell are you supposed to do? You have to make your way. I shrugged angrily and kicked again and spit and felt like hell.

Finally someone stopped, another trucker, and he had his heater on so at least I was warm when he let me off by the campus. It was one-thirty by this time, but since I had to pass Ape Hall anyhow, I went up and listened at Dan's door. I couldn't hear anything. I unlocked it quietly and pushed it open a few inches, until the hall light fell across the bed. It was empty. "That bitch," I said. "That scheming little bitch." I locked the door and walked across the campus, which was dark and cold and empty, to the House, and tried to get to sleep.

What the hell, kid—you got to learn. They get you soon enough anyhow, one way or another. And if they see you trying to make your way, they all get together and gang up on you. All of them. The World.

CHAPTER ELEVEN

I woke up late the next morning—seven-thirty —and still felt lousy. At least part of it was from Pug's gin, I knew. I did not take well to liquor, and only drank with Caroline because I knew it helped her drink, which for her helped everything.

I felt like taking a shower, but gave up the idea when I heard that gang singing in there, acting like a bunch of kids, probably throwing soap and squirting each other with shower nozzles.

I got dressed and went downstairs, got the paper from the lawn and headed for the kitchen. The House did not serve breakfast, but the pledges took turns at morning coffee and toast duty, and there was usually some dry cereal and fruit around. I took black coffee and toast and sat at the empty end of the dining-room table. The story about the kid was on page one, as the anchor at the bottom, by-lined by Andy Rivers, Sports Editor, Midland *Standard*. It wasn't a bad story really. Andy could generally do a fair job of putting a story together if someone dug up the stuff for him. For in spite of his obnoxious ways, he could on occasion show flickering vestiges of intelligence and ability and even, in unguarded moments, of human decency, but he had gone lazy, he had taken the bait, and now was comfortably wriggling on the same hook as everyone else. All he did every day was sit on his ass and write up a few glib paragraphs—chock-full of Magnusian realism—from the stuff I turned in, or that came off the wire, or that the publicity men mimeographed up for him. He hadn't dug up a story of his own or believed a word he wrote in twenty years.

Anyway, the head was:

MOTHER ABSOLVES FOOTBALL STAR IN SON'S ACCIDENTAL DEATH

Timmy Rending, 11, Dies After Freak Practice Accident

He ran a sidebar under an insert head—DANCER SHOCKED, SADDENED BY BOY'S DEATH—with a statement from Dancer about what a great kid Timmy was and how bad he felt, and how he probably wouldn't ever step on a football field again, except that he knew the kid would want him to, and how he hoped in the years ahead he could perform in such a way as would have made Timmy proud of him and the whole team.

I turned to the sports page to check the Townbird story and my practice story. The practice story, naturally, had no by-line, and Andy used the Townbird stuff for his column. I started browsing through them, but didn't get very far. Nothing stirs a Kappa Delt's sympathy more readily than the sight of a brother sitting alone somewhere enjoying his solitude:

"Morning, Jack—how are you? Didn't see you at the meeting last night?"

"Shitty," I said. Obscenity was prohibited by Kappa Delta by-laws, especially at meals. "I've been drinking too much and getting laid too often."

"Getting it regular, eh?"

"Yes," I said. You never knew how the boys would react. Sometimes they'd be so pious they'd blush when you said bathroom, and the next night the same guys would get a couple of beers in them and see who could tell the filthiest jokes to other guys' dates. What really got me was the time one of our brothers got killed, along with his girl, in a crash on the way back from the woods at night; the whole fraternity practiced abstinence for a week.

"Who's the lucky girl, Jack? Maybe she'd have a little left over for some of us peasants. We could sorta fill in when you're busy somewhere else."

"You couldn't fill in for me," I said. "It's the coach's wife, if you're really interested. I've been laying her regular for a year or so now."

"Sure. You gonna try Irvine's wife next?"

"I think she's a little old for me."

One of the guys was stretching to look at my paper. "Hey —that little kid died, eh?"

"That's what the story says."

"He musta really got conked."

"He got kneed in the groin—Dancer lost his head and thought he was in a real game."

"Cut it. Boy, Dancer must feel pretty bad."

"He feels shocked and saddened," I said. "The story there tells all about it." I finished my coffee and was going for seconds when a pledge leaned in from the hall:

"Hey, Jack—you got a call."

"Excuse me, brothers." I went into the hall. If it was Andy at this time of the morning it meant someone from Tech blew up the football stadium.

"Hello, Jack Wyant?—Mr. Davidson. How are you?"

"I'm fine . . . But I don't think I quite remember . . ."

"Have a Royal King!—They're as mild as a smile, gentle as a mountain breeze!"

"Oh, my Christ!"

"Remember now?"

"Of course—how do you do, sir? Where—are you in town?"

"Metro Caf, having a tomato juice cocktail. How's chances of stopping by, saying hello?"

"Sure—sure. Only I—I really wanted to have things a little more set up when you came. I thought it'd be later in the year. School hasn't even started yet and—"

"No strain. Just a friendly visit—get to know our boys, see what they're like. How do I find your place?"

I told him and hung up. It was too late to do anything; I sat down and had another cup of coffee. I couldn't trade back all the Lords in my closet for Royal Kings, or get up all the signs and posters and displays and everything that were supposed to be around. I decided to tell him some of the guys played a practical joke on me—switched all the cigarettes, pulled down all the posters. Besides, school hadn't even started; they couldn't expect me to have done too much yet. The job didn't come out to an awful lot of money over the year, but I didn't really want to lose it. It helped, and it kept me in cigarettes, and I got a lot of pleasure out of sending those reports in.

I watched the window and about ten minutes later saw Davidson pull up in a white Corvette. He carried a square leather brief case, shaped something like a portable typewriter case, and wore a charcoal gray suit and a gray hat. He was a lot younger than I expected, and very clean-cut. I don't think he was even thirty.

We shook hands and I offered him a seat in the living room. I hoped to keep him downstairs, but right away he shook his head.

"How's chances for a little privacy? Business secrets, you know," he said, tapping his brief case. He really was young, real Joe College too—everything except the pipe.

"Well, I don't know . . ."

"You must have a room somewhere. Let's go."

I took him upstairs to the room. The door to the closet wasn't even closed—it was overflowing with cartons of Lords. He sat on a chair without saying anything. I shut the closet casually and sat on the bed.

"Well, Jack—we've been very happy with your work—you showed us a lot of verve, a lot of imagination last year."

"I'm glad you were pleased."

"You were even in the running for our Campus Representative of the Year Award—did you know that?"

"No, sir, I didn't."

"Unfortunately, you were edged out right at the last—but of course you'll have another shot at it this year. How old are you, Jack? You look a little more mature than most of our boys."

"Twenty-five," I said. "I spent a few years in the Coast Guard."

"Ever had any business experience?"

"No, sir. This is the first real job I've ever had."

He sat back in his chair and started patting his pockets. He smiled. He had a real salesman's smile. "I seem to be out of Royal Kings—Boy, what would they say back in New York, heh? Can I bum one of yours?"

"I seem to be out, too, sir."

"No, you're not," he said, still smiling. "I saw a whole batch of them there in your closet."

"They're just empties," I said. "I save the cartons—I use them for display mountings around campus."

"They can't all be empty—here, let's have a look-see." He went over and opened the closet, bending down to shuffle around a bit while I sat hopelessly on the bed and watched. He came up with a pack of Lords in his hand. "Knew they weren't all empties," he said. He opened the

pack and knocked it on his knuckle, pushing a few cigarettes out. He sniffed them. "Bad," he said. "Very bad."
He dropped the whole pack into the trash can. "Here," he
said, reaching inside his jacket. "Try something worth
smoking." He flipped me a cigar. I looked at it. "Go
ahead. Costs fifty cents, tastes fine, and is fully guaranteed
to have less cancer than cigarettes—although of course after
twenty or thirty years your lower lip drops into your lap."
He laughed and lit a cigar himself. I took the wrapper off
mine and lit it.

"Very good," I said.

He sat on the chair again and picked up his brief case,
tapping it deliberately with his index finger. "Now down
to business. Hope you don't mind my bringing the typewriter along. But I'm really loaded down with work—have
to make every minute count."

"Not at all."

He opened the case and turned it around for my in-
spection. "What's your choice, Jack?"

Lined up inside the case, each in its own niche like statues in the wall of some Mexican church, where three bottles: scotch, bourbon, and gin. A covered metal compartment lay on the left side and underneath this were two
glasses and a small bottle of vermouth. Between the necks
of the scotch and the bourbon was nested a bottle of
olives; between the bourbon and the gin, a bottle of onions.
He laughed as I looked, and took the cover off the metal
compartment.

"On a good day they'll last six or eight hours," he said,
pointing to the ice cubes. "What's your color?"

"I don't drink much," I said.

"I don't either. But that doesn't answer the question."

"Scotch."

He poured about four inches over an ice cube and passed
me the glass. He made one for himself. "To the queens."

"The queens . . . ?"

"The people who screw the Royal Kings," he explained.

We drank. It didn't taste very good. I couldn't imagine any liquor tasting good at 8:30 A.M., and my stomach still felt uneasy from the two gins the night before.

He smacked his lips, sat back, rested the glass on his knee. "God, yes—hair of the dog. And now, Jack, it's my uncomfortable duty to inform you that, despite our pleasure, we've been a bit, well . . . *worried* about you."

"Oh," I said.

"Yes. We read all reports very carefully, you know—study them, analyze them . . ."

"If I've been doing anything wrong, sir, I'd be more than happy to—"

"It's your attitude we're concerned about, Jack. For a while there, we thought you might really be taking this whole thing seriously. Of course, I feel much better now. Hah—a whole closet full of Lords! Lords! Christ, wait'll I tell the boys."

"It was a practical joke, sir—the kids in the House switched them on me and—"

"Relax, Jack. That's great—Lords! Say—where do the girls hang out around here? I got in late last night and figured on maybe a little sleep today and then shaking down some tail tonight."

"Midland Hotel," I said.

"For free?"

"It depends. Try the bar . . . Unless you'd like me to fix you up."

"Thanks, but I enjoy finding them myself. Now, on your reports—calm them down a bit, will you? Everyone *knows* you can't be working that hard. Just say you're running a contest once in a while and checking up on the store displays every month or so. Cut out this crap about deans' offices and doctors' offices. Want another drink?—Hey, you've hardly touched it. Drink up."

He poured himself another. "Here, I'll freshen yours. To the queens. Now tell me, I'm interested—why do you go to all the trouble of trading in Royal Kings for Lords?"

I waited a minute, then said, "Pure malice."

"Only we make Lords too—didn't you know that? We make Royal Kings for people who like long mild cigarettes, Lords for people who like short strong cigarettes, Duchess for people who like regular filters, and Viscount for people who like long filters. Same company. Same tobacco for the most part too. Here, have another shot."

"No thanks—really."

"Who'd you think you were screwing, anyhow? No one gives a damn if you're working or not. If we don't pay you, we pay Uncle Sam."

"Somebody must think I'm working."

"Nobody I know."

"Oh," I said. I was sort of disappointed.

"Ha!" He finished his drink and put the glass back in the brief case. He stood up, waiting for mine. I took a deep breath and finished it. He put my glass back, too, and closed the case. "Man, I'm beat. I'll send in a report saying that you're true blue and doing a great job for us out here. And if the girls come through tonight, I might even recommend you for Campus Representative of the Year. So don't quit, even though I've killed the romance for you. Remember, romantics die of consumption in garrets; it's us realists who get the chauffeurs and mansions. Here—" He took something out of his pocket, licked it, and stuck it on my desk. "Official badge," he said. "Keep up the good work." It was a British postage stamp, with a picture of Queen Elizabeth. He doffed his hat and left, swinging the brief case through the door.

The drinks made my head and stomach even worse than when I woke up, so I took a double dose of Fizrin. I could never see what anybody saw in drinking when all it did was make you feel rotten the next day. It's pretty hard, though, trying to go through life without drinking. Somebody is always shoving a glass at you, and boy, that glass is the sign, the symbol. If you don't take it, you're really thumbs down, and everybody starts feeling sorry for you, figuring something must be wrong with you or that you're some kind of Baptist or Mormon or something. Or they think that maybe you're looking down on them, criticizing them, and drinkers are very sensitive to criticism. Just give them the slightest hint and watch their hackles rise. No matter what you say, they won't believe that you just don't *want* a drink. After a while, I started telling people how my father was an alcoholic, and that's why I didn't drink, but that only got me sermons about how nobody with any real will power ever becomes an alcoholic, and that it isn't inheritable and that you just have to know when to stop, and that as long as you don't really need the drink, you're all right. Meanwhile dribbling down their chins.

I picked up my mail on the way out—a letter from my father—and headed for the practice field. It was ten o'clock; morning practice started at nine-thirty. I hoped to get hold of Dan during the break, so I could talk to him about at least one of the things that bothered me, which was how he was reacting to the kid's dying. As well as I knew Dan, I had no idea how it would affect him. Sometimes he seems very sentimental and moral, and other times things don't affect him at all. They could be happening all around him, but it'd be like he didn't even realize it, didn't even care. I didn't want him getting all worked up over the kid, and wanted to let him know how he should feel about it before he got any ideas himself—and even more important, before the White Goddess of the YWCA gave him any. Which was the other thing I wanted to talk to Dan about. Her.

The walk in the air helped, and I felt a little better when I got to the gym, and didn't even mind having to stop twice to direct beanied pubertarians to the library and the administration building. I went through the catacombs and past the locker rooms, waved to Nick, who was chewing a cigar and waxing helmets, and walked down the ramp to the practice field. Piney Savage had the backfields working signals, Joe Minotti was running the guards on pullout plays, and Sam Bassey had somebody throwing into defensive pass patterns. And in the middle, above all the movement and the shouts and the chanted signals, Pug stood on top of his wooden stand with his binoculars around his neck and with Jerry Dinsmoor alongside writing in his notebook.

I walked part way down the edge of the field and sat on the grass and opened my father's letter. He didn't write often; he was primarily a talker and never had much to say when confronted with the perplexing challenges of written communication. He used lined paper and wrote very large.

Dear Jack,

How are you and all your firends at school, getting along ok I hope. There is not much news to report I thought you might just like to hear a little from the folks before the school and everything starts again so we could all wish you good luck. Your mother you know especilly is very proud of you as I am too and all the family, we hope and know you will do very well again this year son. Your aunt Tessie is bothered again with the Bursitus in her shoulder but will be ok Im sure. We like to hear from you but know how busy you are and school comes first, so write when you get a chance so we all know you are well. Do your best son, it is a great opportunty to have and you are very lucky, make the best of it.

Love from all,
Your Father

I folded the letter up and put it in my pocket. Actually, I enjoyed hearing from him. I liked the letters, liked the illiteracies and the misspellings and the little pep talk he always worked in at the end. At least he was human. For everything else he lacked, the guy was a human being, and I had not found myself bumping into any great horde of them around the university campus.

I tried to watch practice a little, but without much success. The morning had been cool, but the sun was strong by this time, warming the grass and drugging the air with the syrupy odor of turf. I began to feel drowsy, and thought longingly of being able to stretch out and sleep for an hour or so. I'm sure it was Davidson's scotch, because I'm never tired, never sleep at all during the day, no matter how little I've had the night before. But that scotch had really set me off. I even felt kind of hot and lightheaded sitting in the sun. And when I saw Pug calmly and methodically lift the binoculars to pull the strap over his head and hand them to Jerry Dinsmoor, and then turn around and reach his foot back to the top rung of the wooden ladder and start climbing down, I was not even awake enough or sharp enough to react to what was happening. I just stared at him as he stretched first one leg and then the other behind and below to the next rung of the ladder, watched as he turned squarely, like a soldier off duty who had relaxed enough to lose his drill-field stiffness but not so much as to lose its neatness and precision. And again maybe it was the scotch, especially on top of last night's gin, Pug's gin, that made me for the first time think of him coming toward me in his University sweatshirt and peaked cap as the husband of the woman I had been in bed with twelve hours before. I stared at him marching toward me without being able to react in any way except to try to loosen my mind enough so I would be able to see him once more the way I always saw him, as a nice guy, almost a friend, a good coach, and not at all connected with Caroline, or even with the gin I got from her. And then, before I got my mind working, he was right in front of me, stopping the way he had started, with the relaxed precision of the off-duty soldier, and then everything focused all at once, painfully, and I realized I wasn't even sitting on the grass any more. I was lying, stretched out, my head on my hand, my elbow digging into the grass. I clambered up clumsily, swiping at my pants, as if somehow in light of the sudden clarification of mind nothing mattered as much as getting a few blades of grass off my trousers.

"He's not here," Pug said, stating a simple point of information, not even raising his voice over the shouts of the players running up and down the field behind him. That was just like him, marching dramatically up to you, and then doing nothing more than making a flat, low-keyed statement like that. Pug was a quiet, undemonstrative man, and the quieter he got, the more you knew he was bubbling inside, the raw acid silently eroding away whatever effect those pills were supposed to have on him. He stared at me closely, but seemed not to see me jumping up or swiping at my pants. He seemed to be staring without anything else around to weaken the directness of his gaze.

"Where is he?" I asked.

"You're the one who is supposed to know that. I'm being paid to show him how to hold the ball when he runs, and you're being paid to make sure that he is here so that I can give him the ball and let him run."

I was already moving. Pug did not try to stop me, or wave, or say anything else. He stood on the grass in his sweatshirt and peaked cap, his hands on his hips, his face calm and steady, watching me run.

CHAPTER TWELVE

Dan was in his room. He was sleeping when I knocked, and he came to the door in his woolen pajamas. He wasn't fully awake; he stared at me blearily, holding the knob. He didn't say anything, didn't even look surprised or angry. When I pushed the door open a little more, he stepped back with it as if it did not occur to him to let go of the knob, and I walked in. He closed the door. He watched, still bleary, as I sat in the basket chair, and then, still without saying anything, he walked back to the bed in his pajamas and bare feet and sat down. He didn't look good. From the way he looked, he might have got home last night with just enough energy and clearness of mind left to throw his clothes off—they were still on the floor— and get his pajamas on and get into bed. That clean, smooth, alert face with its perfect features looked somehow askew, a little gray around the eyes, a little sagged and dried out.

"Good morning," I said.

"Morning."

"I just came from practice," I said.

He said nothing.

"Everyone's there," I said. "You should see them going

at it, running up and down the field, practicing signals, getting all set for the big game tomorrow."

He stared at me sleepily, his eyes red, half-closed, then turned away and looked at his pillow, his bed.

"How come you're not there?" I asked.

"Because you knocked," he said, turning back to me. "You woke me up."

"At practice," I said. "At practice."

"I'm tired."

"I thought you were staying home to go to bed at ten last night—that'd give you twelve hours by now."

He said nothing.

"Although, of course, maybe you went out last night. After all, why not? You're a free man. You don't owe anybody anything for the few lousy thousand dollars a year you're costing them—to say nothing about your father's new car or—"

"I'm tired. I'm going back to sleep."

"What about practice?"

"I'm not going to practice."

He lay down again, pulling the blanket over him. I never knew a guy who slept under more covers or with more clothes. "When are you going to wake up?" I asked.

"I don't know. Leave me alone."

"Did you get in any knife fights last night?"

"No."

I realized then that he probably didn't even know that the kid had died, but I didn't say anything. He closed his eyes and either pretended to go to sleep or else went to sleep—I couldn't tell which at first. I sat for a few minutes, looking at him, listening to him. I decided he was really asleep and went downstairs to the dorm phone. It was just time for the break at practice, and I got Pug in his office.

"He's in his room," I told him. "He found out about that kid and it really broke him up."

"He's not supposed to be in his room. He's supposed to be at practice."

"He's taking it pretty bad—I think it'd be a good idea just to let him stew it out. He'll be all right then. I'll stay with him."

"You should have known about this this morning. You should have figured it was going to happen before it happened and been there."

"It's nothing, I tell you. He'll be okay. Just leave him with me."

He hung up.

I went back to the room. Dan was curled up, his knees in his stomach, the blanket pulled over him, almost covering his face. He was dead asleep.

I looked around for something to read and found *Huckleberry Finn* and picked out a few sections from the middle that I liked and read them again, but my head bothered me and I didn't feel much like reading. I'm a pretty sporadic reader generally, and only read when I feel like it. I usually go through a book in a couple of hours, though, even a big one, and manage to read two or three books a week that way, which is roughly ten times what the average Kappa Delt reads. The guys at the House, though, are convinced I never read anything, not even textbooks, because they never see me mooning around for weeks at a time with the same book in my hand. When a Kappa Delt sits down to read a book, everybody in the House knows it, it's an occasion, and for the next month the guy is more or less on exhibition, with all the guys watching him in awe as he sits around slack-jawed, following his finger across the lines, moving his lips. Dancer was probably even worse. I don't know when he started *Huckleberry Finn*, but according to the torn-off corner of a *Life* magazine cover he was using as a placemark, he was on page twelve. They read a novel a week in that American lit course, and even if Dan made it through *Huckleberry Finn,* I couldn't quite picture him getting past *Moby Dick* the next week and following it up with *The Ambassadors, Sister Carrie, The Sound and the Fury* and *The Grapes of Wrath.* And worst of all, if he did take the course—if his friend down-town managed to talk him into it faster than I could talk him out of it—he would actually try to read all the books. Some of the guys I had last year—like Chuck Janowski—were no trouble at all. They didn't want to do anything. When they had a theme to write on "My Favorite Character from Fiction" or "The Need for Higher Admission Standards," or "My Idea of the Function of a University," they'd just let me write it for them. When they had a test, they'd take the sheet of information I'd work up and try to memorize it, or at least copy it on the inside of their cuffs or something. They didn't care whether they understood anything or not, or learned anything. If they got past the exam, they were eternally grateful. And in their big lecture classes, where there were hundreds of students and the in-structor didn't know anyone and gave only carefully steri-lized true-or-false IBM machine-graded exams, they'd be more than happy to let me go and take the exam for them.

Not Dancer. From the beginning he had in him some monstrous urge to knowledge, which was probably why May was able to make the idealistic plant bloom again this year with so little watering, because the seed was al-ready there, the seed which all last year I had realistically tried to choke off. Dan was so bad he even used to lecture Chuck and the other guys in our group, giving them pep talks about doing their own work and trying to learn. For a shy boy who doesn't say much to other people, especially about their own business, Dan really had a bug about school. The other guys started calling him The Old Profes-

sor and Einstein, but Dan has the sense of humor of a
true zealot, and he'd just shrug and say, "Okay. Only I
don't see what you came here for if you don't want to
learn." Finally I told him to lay off. He was getting so
moral about everything I was afraid he'd sound off some-
day to the wrong people. He'd do things like that if you
weren't careful, lacking, as he did, the intelligence to make
discreet judgments in complex situations.

I finally won Dan over to my system—and only partially,
at that—by first letting him go ahead by himself in his
courses, the way he wanted to, until he screwed up so
hopelessly he was willing to listen to me. And then I still
had to convince him that it was really his work we were
turning in, that I was just going over it to brush it up a
bit. Of course, this was a lot more bother. The other guys
didn't even look at the things before turning them in, and
I'd knock out a solidly passing but unsuspicious theme for
them in about fifteen minutes; it'd take hours with Dan.
First of all, he'd insist on writing the thing himself, so it'd
be his own work, and then I'd have to go over it with him,
line by line, explaining every change. This took some doing. Most people think that it's easy correcting and changing things that are really bad, but Dancer had a way with
the English language that taxed your faith in the descrip-
tive powers of formal grammar. Once he wrote a theme de-
scribing his home that began:

> My brothers room in unorganized, coverid with debris,
> an dusty: Moms and Dads room is used only at night,
> (for sleeping,) and so theirfor not much pride is con-
> nected by anybody with it's apparance, (Its dark at
> night anyway); and, finally my room is extremely dis-
> organized and in proper, and it to is, guilty of being
> dusty.

Thankfully, this was the last theme he insisted on turning in without my okay. Mr. Manquero, who isn't much for football players anyhow and who prides himself on his wry humor, failed it with the bland comment, "Foul and Gross Blunders Mar This Work!"

"What does he mean?" Dancer wanted to know.

"He means it's lousy," I explained. "Stinking, bad, crummy, no good."

"Oh," he said. Quietly. "Oh."

But even after he learned his lesson, he never went along easily, the way the others did. He'd get bothered by the way I'd tear his themes apart and would go over them himself, after I finished and without telling me, and make his own corrections. But when the solid Cs I had been getting him started turning into Fs, I got suspicious. He said he didn't mean to criticize my writing; I wrote fine, but he wanted to get some of his own ideas into the paper. I'm still amazed Manquero didn't catch on, because Dan's themes would become astounding montages: a paragraph of good solid, unexciting C work, followed by one like that description of Dan's house. But I long ago lost my faith in the grading of freshmen English instructors. Their brains have over the years leaked away into illegible red marks in margins.

"What does a good-looking kid like you gotta worry about learning things for?" I'd tell Dan whenever he'd start getting moral again.

But then he'd just sulk. "Sure, people look at me and say there goes a guy with brains, a smart guy. All right, so I look smart. I got through high school with that look. But that look don't ace many decks. When you come right down to it, I ain't too smart."

"You'll get by. Stop worrying about it."

"But I can't learn anything that way."

The trouble, of course, was that he couldn't learn any-

thing any way. The harder he tried, the worse it was. When
every other freshman just took one look at the English
vocabulary list and threw it away, Dan decided to memorize it. For a while he'd go around saying, "That was a
cataclysmic rain we had last night, wasn't it?" Or he'd
write in a theme that a girl was "kind of pretty with a
sharp build and a cute face and vivacious, meditative
eyes."

Our biggest troubles were the themes they had to write
in class, and the surprise quizzes. One day a history prof
got sore when somebody asked him whether the Civil War
was in the seventeenth or eighteenth century, and he gave
them a one-question quiz. That night Dan came to me
with that vivacious, meditative look in his eyes, and I could
tell he was going through the birth pangs of knowledge
again. "What are the exclusive dates for the eighteenth
century?" he asked.

"You mean inclusive?"

"Yeah. The teacher asked us to write them down. He
said he wanted to see if we knew them."

"What'd you write?"

"Eighteen hundred."

"One-eight-oh-oh?"

"Yeah."

"You said he asked for the inclusive dates."

"I know—I was wondering how I did. I guess I'll have
to just wait and see."

"Yeah," I said. "Let's wait and see. Look, I got an idea.
You call me George, all right, and I'll call you Lennie. Do
you like rabbits?"

"What?"

"Never mind."

"What do you mean? What are you talking about?"

"Nothing, nothing. Forget it."

The thing that got me about Dancer's intellectual ambitions was that they were invented by Red Warwick. In high school Dancer was content just to play football and baseball and basketball, probably without opening a book in four years and certainly without feeling any lack thereby. He accepted his A in senior English, for instance—after spending half the year reading *Julius Caesar* and the other half pasting pictures in the yearbook—as only his due. But then one day Red Warwick materialized out of the surrounding mountains, one of the pack of twenty or thirty scouts and coaches who materialized the same way, who followed a star over Humbolt, Pennsylvania, bringing with them their academic frankincense and General Motors myrrh. And although Red came through with pretty much the best offer—after Benny and Andy and Pug had responded to that desperate midnight call by brow-beating Irvine into line—Red would have lost the prize anyhow if he had not managed to get through to Dancer the way he did, to get through to this incredibly stupid and gifted athlete who had not learned ten facts in his life from his teachers, and not only convince him that he could become an engineer or an accountant, but also somehow ignite in him a spark of pure and unfaked intellectual curiosity—giving us the bloodcurdling image of a freshman football coach who'd be willing to burn down the Widener and Alexandrian libraries together to get a dependable defensive guard, achieving out of sheer greed what not a single one of the kid's dedicated teachers had ever been able to achieve in any way whatsoever.

And so Dan had come to us, had come out of the mountains and coal mines of Humbolt, Pennsylvania, to do reluctantly the one thing he could do really well, but which he did only because he had to do that thing in order to get what he mistakenly thought was an honest chance to do the one thing he actually wanted to do.

I was asleep like the proverbial concierge, I guess, asleep

on the chair with the turned-over copy of *Huckleberry Finn* in my lap when I woke so suddenly, woke so frightened, that I knocked the book half across the room and was on my feet before I even realized I was awake. The room was absolutely silent, but I knew I had heard something, and that what I had heard had wakened me and frightened me. And then Dan, curled up tight on the bed, stiffened and shot his legs straight down under the covers, the soft and indistinct ball snapping rigid like a pocket knife, and screamed again.

I stood and watched him. I thought sure he would wake up. He writhed on the bed, twisted, punched his pillow; then he relaxed, moaning softly; and then muttered something that sounded like words without being words, a whole string of tormented and incomprehensible sounds, muttered with a kind of desperate pleading, a formless agony. And then he screamed again and kicked and sat upright, his eyes wide and unseeing, like open holes, like pits chucked out of flesh, looking right at me without knowing I was there, and then he shook his head slowly, sadly, moaning, his lips wet now, the corners of that straight, handsome mouth filling with spittle, and then he fell back. He did not lay back or lower himself, but just dropped back as if someone had pulled out the single bolt holding him upright; he fell back the way a loaded sack set on its bottom would tip back; and then he was quiet. I waited a few minutes, standing, watching. He was motionless again, and asleep.

The concierge, the nursemaid, did not sleep this time. I felt sorry for Dancer sleeping under that blanket, even in his sleep pulling it up over him as if he were freezing. I knew he had never been hurt playing football, had never been hurt playing anything, and that that wasn't what started the nightmares. One time I asked him—I was the only one who knew about them—and he said he got hurt riding a bike as a kid, hitting something and bouncing off the seat into the handlebars, getting it in the groin. But I don't think that started them. Too many kids get hurt like that, get hurt one way or another, without getting nightmares for the rest of their lives. And the nightmares hadn't even started until right at the end in high school, until almost ten years after the accident on the bike.

"When you stopped liking it," I said.

"Around there."

"Maybe that has something to do with it."

"I don't think so," he said.

"Are you afraid during the games?"

"No."

"Right before? Right after?"

"No."

"Just when you sleep, just when you dream—is that the only time?"

"Yes."

"What do you dream?"

"Everything," he said. "All sorts of things," but then he wouldn't talk about it any more.

I found out in the first place only by accident. One night last year I had come over to his room to work with him, but saw no light under the door and was about to leave—last year if Dan's room was dark at night, it meant he was sleeping—when I heard him scream inside. I knocked and woke him up. He came to the door shivering, although he wore a heavy sweater over his woolen pajamas and had been sleeping under a couple of blankets in a steam-heated room. And that's when he told me about it. I stayed with him most of the night, talking with him, keeping him company, until finally at three or four in the morning he was ready to try to go back to sleep.

It was almost noon now, and although my head still hurt, my stomach felt a little better and I was hungry. I was trying to decide whether I should sneak out and hope to get back before he woke up, or wake him and take him with me, when someone knocked.

Dan did not stir.

I went to the door and opened it quietly. It was Pug.

"Where's Dan?" He spoke flatly, staring in at me through the half-opened door. He wore a lifeless brown suit with a big figured tie that had gone out of style ten years ago. He never looked good in a suit and tie. The suits never fit, always ballooning at the wrong places, making him look small and insignificant within the folds, uncomfortable, the way you'd imagine some sort of ineffectual little man would look, only then you noticed his face, tight, hard, controlled, calm—anything in the world but ineffectual.

I stepped out to the hall and closed the door behind me. "He's asleep," I said. "He was all worked up and I gave him some stuff I got down at the drugstore."

"I want to talk to him."

"I think it'd be better if he slept it off."

"I think it'd be better if I talked to him."

He stared at me steadily, his head pushed forward, almost on his chest. I stood right in front of him, pressed against the door. He had not stepped back to give me room.

"All right," I said. "But don't mention the kid—it'll just start him off again."

"What happened to the kid, anyhow? Was the crap in the paper straight?"

"Yes. The bump on the head did it."

Pug shrugged, not as if to shrug anything off, but irritably, futilely. "Somebody should've got him to a doctor. Poor slob."

"I know," I said.

"Christ, I can't worry about everything. I can't worry about every gooddamn kid who wants to come down and watch us." He shrugged again, the same way, and then looked at me, stared right into my eyes, and said, a little impatiently: "Can I go in, now?"

Dan was still asleep on the bed, still curled up under the covers, as if his whole body were a tight fist. Pug stood over him, looking down, without touching him or moving. He spoke firmly: "Dan! Wake up."

Dan lay still, his eyes closed.

I stepped in front of Pug and shook Dan's shoulders. "Wake up, Dan. Pug's here."

Dan came out of it slowly. He blinked his eyes, and I spoke to him again. He sat up and looked around, pushing the covers away absently, moving his head as if his neck were stiff. At least he looked better than he had when I woke him earlier.

"He's not out of it yet," I said. I stepped back, out of the way.

"I'll wait," Pug said.

Finally Dancer looked at Pug. He did not show any surprise, at least not to Pug, but he was surprised. He knew that Pug did not often come on campus, did not often speak to his players, even on the field, let alone come to their rooms to talk to them.

"Hello," Dan said.

"Are you awake?"

"Yes."

"Do you feel all right?"

"Yes."

"You should have been at practice this morning."

Dancer said nothing. I tried to catch Pug's eye. I wanted to tell him with my look, my eyes, not to mention the kid, but he gave no sign of noticing me. I could just as well not have been in the room; the two of them did not take their eyes off each other. Dancer was still sitting on the edge of the bed, Pug—looking, except for his face, like the owner of a variety store in a badly fitting suit—was still standing over him.

"We don't give excuses from practice," Pug said. "Everybody is supposed to be there every day."

Then I noticed the desperation in Pug's voice, the quiet, agonized desperation. And realized what it must have meant to him to come on campus, to come up to the dorm, to knock on Dancer's door, what it meant to this man who had to fight all his life to get what he wanted, but who never had fought this way, never had come pleading, asking, begging—who had always fought desperately, but never with this kind of desperation.

"I'll be there this afternoon," Dancer said. He did not say it apologetically. It was a statement.

"There's no practice this afternoon. I announced that yesterday. We never have practice Friday afternoon."

"I forgot."

"Our next required attendance is tonight at the rally. And then tomorrow we have a game. Did you forget that too? Would you like me to come over and remind you of all required attendances?"

"I'll be there tonight," Dancer said. He too spoke quietly, but almost dully, without the intensity that stiffened Pug's speech.

"That'll be a real kindness."

Dancer said nothing.

"I haven't got time enough to go around reminding everybody of everything," Pug said, nearing the edge now, the desperation showing through more and more. "I have a lot of things to do. I have a whole squad, fifty-three guys to worry about. Maybe some people think some of those guys are worth more trouble than others, but as far as I'm concerned there are fifty-three guys to worry about, to take care of. I don't have the time to chase after people and give lectures and remind them of things. And I don't have the stomach to ask people to play; I *let* them play—if they're good enough, if they want to enough. When it comes time that I have to ask you to do something, I'll ask you to leave, to go. Remember that. That's the only kind of asking I do."

Dancer said nothing.

"All right," Pug said. "All right. We'll see you tonight." He closed the door behind him.

Dancer remained sitting on the edge of the bed. His expression had not changed, and I still could just as well not have been there.

"You should have said you were sorry," I said.

Dan shrugged. He seemed finally awake now. His eyes were clear. "What time is it?"

"Almost noon. Are you hungry?"

"Yes."

"I'll buy you a hamburger. We got things to talk about."

CHAPTER THIRTEEN

We went off campus, to Ginger's Cafe on Fifth. I had one hamburger and Dan had three. Then he had two pieces of pie and a second strawberry malted. He said little; he listened while I told him about the kid. I even got a copy of the *Standard* and showed him the stories, but he still didn't say anything, not even when he read his own statement. And he didn't look surprised, or sorry, or even uncomfortable. He didn't complain, as I was sure he would, about us printing a statement that he didn't make. Finally he said, "Too bad," but even then I couldn't tell if he was just saying it because he felt he ought to say it, or whether he actually felt bad but didn't know how to show it, or didn't want to show it. Dan was hard to get to know. I don't think I ever understood him, ever truly had any idea how he felt, how his mind worked, what drove it. Dan never lied. He never played anything phony, never tried to fool anyone, and you would think someone like that would be easy to see through. Of all the people I've known, he was, except for my father, the only one I believed to be honest and sincere, absolutely and completely honest and sincere, and yet he was the only one who always managed in the final moment to elude me, the only one I never could understand or feel I had in hand.

We walked back to his dorm. It was about one o'clock,
and I knew I had a pretty long day—and night—ahead of
me, but I wasn't going to let Dancer out of sight, if I could
help it, until he suited up for the game tomorrow. Maybe
I went around a lot picking up deals and getting away
with whatever I could, but still I had some pride and liked
to think I could be counted on to do a job when I was supposed to do it. My first two days of nursemaiding Dan
weren't too successful, I realized—although thankfully no
one else realized it to quite the extent that I did—what
with a knife fight the first day and his staying out all night
and sleeping through practice the next. There would be no
more of that. I didn't take to the idea of someone like
Benny or Andy being able to say I screwed up, or of losing
battles to someone like May. And I didn't like the idea of
letting Pug down.

"Are you just gonna hang around all day?" Dancer asked
as we moved across campus. A lot of the freshmen stared;
they had seen Dancer's picture in the papers and seeing him
actually walk by, in the flesh, was probably the first great
thrill of their college careers. And I guess the fact that the
kid he ran into died gave his fame a little fillip.

"Sure," I said. "I got nothing to do." We went up to his
room and I sat in the basket chair. "What about you?" I
said. "What are you going to do?"

"Sleep."

"You've been sleeping all morning," I reminded him.

"I'm tired."

"What are you doing—resting up so you can joy-ride
around all night again tonight? There's a game tomorrow,
you know. Look, Dan, just between you and me—what the
hell time did you get in last night?"

He shrugged. He was taking off his clothes, getting
ready to put on his woolies. It was the middle of the day

now, the September sun was directly overhead, and the room was warm.

"I would honestly like to know," I said. "Just for my own information. I won't tell a soul."

"Seven o'clock."

"Seven o'clock! Christ, it must have been light by then. Did anybody see you?"

"It was just getting light. I saw somebody else, though."

"Who?"

"Pug."

"*Pug?*" I think I was shouting by this time. "Pug? What'd you do—stop and say hello to him?"

"No. He didn't even see us."

"Are you positive?"

"Yeah. We were in the car, turning a corner, and it was still pretty dark. He wasn't even looking. He was just walking along the street toward his house."

"Christ—at seven o'clock in the morning!"

"Yeah. I wondered what he was doing out so early."

"So late. He was watching those goddamn films all night." Good God, I thought. No wonder he was so near the edge with Dan this morning. And no wonder Caroline bitched.

"I kinda feel bad," Dan said. "Him working like that."

"And you missing practice," I said.

"I know."

"Well, then you should've at least said you were sorry. Anyhow, just don't pull that again. Play good tomorrow. He'll forgive you."

He had his pajamas on now. "I'm gonna sleep. Are you gonna just stay here?"

"Yeah," I said. "You forgot your sweater."

"I don't want it. What're you gonna do all afternoon?"

"Read," I said. "Improve my mind."

"All I got is that *Huckleberry Finn*."

"I know. I was reading it this morning."

"You like it?"

"I like it fine."

He got into bed, tucking his feet under the covers. "I thought the writing was kinda rough in spots myself. But that Huck's okay. Sometimes he was pretty mean to the colored fellow, but he wasn't really mean underneath."

"I thought you were only up to page twelve."

"No, I finished it." He paused to let the impressiveness of his achievement sink in. "I'm going through it again. I think I missed some things. Some of the jokes and stuff."

"It's possible," I admitted.

He pulled up the covers and rolled toward the wall, and I started to read, figuring he had dropped right off. One thing about athletes, you can usually count on them all the way for eating and sleeping. But about ten minutes later he sat up: "Mind if I turn on the radio?" He found some hillbilly music and lay on his back this time, his arm bent over his eyes. After a bit he said, without getting up or removing his arm: "Rough about that kid, heh?"

"It wasn't your fault."

"I know."

"Don't start worrying about it now. It was an accident. It could just as easily have been you." Which was of course just about the stupidest thing I could have said. That's what you get for not thinking, for just saying what comes naturally into your mind without planning out every word ahead of time. Christ, if you're not on top of things every minute, you're nowhere. Anyhow, I couldn't see how to go about making it better, so I kept quiet. Dan was quiet a few minutes, too, and then he just said:

"Yeah."

That was all. A little while later I could hear him breathing; he was finally out. I left the radio on because I was afraid he'd wake up if I turned it off, and read most of the afternoon, with Ernest Tubbs and Hank Arnold providing background music. Along the way I caught Hal Winston's local sports show, on which he interviewed Pug.

"Well, coach, with the big first game coming up, the annual classic tomorrow, do you think it's going to be a battle between your great offense with Dancer leading the way and Tech's fine defensive platoon, or do you think it's going to be one of those traditional knock-down drag-out affairs between two well-balanced clubs with the breaks and old Lady Luck throwing the dice to decide who's going to emerge victorious?"

"Yes . . . I think that's it, Hal."

"How do you see it then, Pug?"

"Well, it's going to be a tough game, Hal . . ."

The hillbilly music returned and I finished the book. I found someone down the hall with a typewriter he wasn't using, and wrote up my story on the rally, and on today's practice, and then went back to Dan's room. He was still asleep. I woke him at five, and since I couldn't afford to buy him supper, too, just to keep him near by, I invited him to the House. We were allowed to bring guests to dinner, especially nonaffiliated guests, because Giffling and the boys were always hot for new recruits. You were supposed to notify the house manager six months ahead of time or something, but I knew they wouldn't mind if I showed up with Dancer. Every fraternity on campus had tried to get him last year. He didn't like the idea of having to like a whole bunch of guys, though, of having to promise to like them before he even knew them. No one else did either, I guess, but Dancer was the kind of guy who worried about things like that.

I think Giffling had been sitting around all day working up the lecture he was going to give me, because the minute I walked in he got up from the president's chair—we had a big leather armchair near the fireplace that only the president could sit in, on which each president's name was inscribed in indelible ink when he left, later to be carefully circled in black when he died—and put aside his *Playboy* magazine and was heading for me with that pious Presbyterian look on his face, his hand a little forward, ready for my sleeve, when he saw Dancer.

"Well, Jack! Hello! How are you?" He even shook my hand.

"Dan Danciewitz," I said, although I knew damn well he knew who it was, and Giffling shook his hand, too, his eyes fluttering. "I brought him for supper," I said.

"Dinner," Giffling said, pumping Dan's hand. "We're honored to have you, Dan."

"Thanks," Dan mumbled. I think he was already sorry he had come. I felt sorry I had to bring him. "There's a message for you upstairs," Giffling said. "You just leave Dan with me—I'll introduce him around."

He had Dan by the sleeve and was leading him over to three guys on the couch as I went upstairs. I read the note a couple of times, then tore it off the door and went over to the phone, reading it again:

> Coaches wife called—said had material
> for story on Coaches family life that
> you'd be interested in. Call bet.
> 3–5 or after 6.

"Mrs. Walters? This is Jack Wyant, reporter for the Midland—"

"It's all right. He's not here. Jack—he knows."

"He does?"

"Yes, I'm sure he does. He hasn't said anything really, only I'm sure he knows. He didn't come home until this morning, but he must have seen something around the house. I'm sure he knows someone was here."

"Does he know who?"

"I don't know. He was pretty calm, the way he is, and I couldn't tell if he just doesn't care or he doesn't want to show it or if he's just so worried about the game tomorrow that he hasn't got time to get bothered."

"Maybe we ought to cut it out—at least for a while."

"He has to be at the rally tonight—can you come over then?"

"I have to cover it for the paper."

"I don't think we have to stop, Jack. I don't think he even cares. I really don't. I was on the verge of just telling him all about it this morning."

"Christ, don't do that!"

"I don't think it'd make any difference."

"Well, I do. Look—I'll try to sneak over tonight, while the rally's on. All right? I won't be able to stay—just a few minutes, so we can talk. Don't say anything to him before then."

"All right."

Everyone was sitting around the table waiting to begin when I got downstairs, and I hurried over to the chair saved for me. Dan was sitting next to Giffling. Guests never sat near the guys who brought them; they were supposed to mingle with the brothers. I didn't even notice who I was next to, but the guy on my right poked my elbow.

"Hi, Jack."

It was Mr. Manquero, looking as dark and somber as always. He never smiled much; he always gave the impression of being pretty worried about the future of man.

"Why, hello," I said. "Hello." Every once in a while the House invited a faculty member for dinner to give the place a little tone, and Giffling usually put them next to me.

Before we had a chance to say anything else, Giffling was tapping his water glass.

"Tonight we will hear Grace said by Brother Wyant. Brother Wyant . . ."

He smiled at me, waiting for me to get up. I gave him a dirty look, but then I got up and he sat down.

"Thank you, O Lord, and bless," I said, looking around at all the tops of heads, "not only this substantial and nutritious meal, but also the wholesome youth who have here congregated in holy Brotherhood to partake of it. Amen."

"Very touching," Manquero said after we started on the soup.

"I try to make it sound sincere."

He nodded, "I see you brought the murderer with you."

"It wasn't his fault," I said. "It was an accident."

"You're quite right. He's just the accomplice, the dupe. I liked the way you people handled it in the paper. I'm always fascinated by the way the monster uses everything. Every kid in the country could get killed playing football, and the next day there'd be stories about what a wholesome way they found to die."

"It was an accident," I said. "A rare and unfortunate accident." The trouble with someone like Manquero was that once they got hot on something, like football, they lost all sense of reason. It seemed to me that anyone with as perverted an idea of what life was really like as Manquero had, wouldn't end up writing much of a novel—which was what Manquero always said he was doing. Although maybe he figured that as an English teacher he more or less had to sound off about football. He probably sneaked into the stadium every Saturday with a disguise on. He probably hadn't missed a game in years.

"I hear we might have a good team this year."

"We might," I said.

"Well, I hope so. For Irvine's sake—the son of a bitch. He wanted a big team, and now maybe he'll be happy."

"He didn't want it," I said. "He just can't buck Benny

and Andy and all the Birds. If Irvine had his way, he'd outlaw football and burn down the stadium."

Manquero laughed. "You know how old Irvine got the presidency?—By promising the regents a winning team in three years."

"I don't believe it. He's been fighting Benny ever since he took over."

"Rub the clouds out of your eyes, Jack. He pretends he's fighting Benny, so he can keep the eggheads happy by blaming him for everything. Only that's not the way it is, Jack. Irvine works harder for the football team than Pug does. Christ, when he needed a new dean a few years back, he managed to find him in a week. It took him four solid months—and I mean solid; he hardly did a damn thing else the whole time—to find and hire Pug."

That got me sore. "For Christ's sake, it's not Irvine," I said. "What can he do with Benny and the Birds and the alumni on his neck all the time, and with Andy bitching in his column all year long whenever we got a crummy team, and telling everybody how good they are upstate, which means what a good school they are and what a crummy school we are? What can he do when Magnus and the goddamn regents and the legislature vomit money for football players but won't let him build a new chem building? How the hell can he buck stuff like that?"

"By pretending he's a man, perhaps. Or maybe even by throwing out everybody on the football team with an IQ under seventy, which should take care of most of them."

"There are some bright guys on the squad," I said.

"Sure, like that Phi Bete they had about a hundred years ago and haven't stopped talking about yet. They should've put him in a bottle. You know, Jack, maybe you ought to just move into Ape along with the rest of them. You're practically one of the boys anyhow."

"Except I pay my own rent."

"True. And you don't walk around with one of those folded-over spiral notebooks stuck in your hip pocket. That's the way to spot an athlete, you know—the notebook in his hip pocket, and the stub pencil he writes in it with. Some of them use the same book all four years, for English, history, economics, biology, the theory of play, everything, all in a few scribbled pages of a spiral notebook, written with a stub pencil. Do you know what I say to myself every time I see one of those mastodons ambling around campus. I say there but for the grace of Benny Johnson goes a couple of thousand books for the library, there goes a lab full of miscroscopes, there goes a fine young physics instructor. And then when I look at the stadium I just turn sick. I can't count that high. I can't conceive of stupidity on that kind of scale."

"You have to buck the other schools," I said. "They all do it."

"Cut it, Jack. Next you'll be telling me football helps pay for new classrooms."

"Anyhow, it's not Irvine's fault."

Manquero shrugged. "You got your story and I got mine."

He chatted with some of the other guys during the rest of the meal, and we didn't say much more to each other. Once when he was talking in class about being self-educated, I asked him how you went about doing it, and he said you found somebody to drink beer with who read the same books you did and disagreed with you about everything, which is all right, I guess—only if Manquero was the guy you found he'd just stop talking to you after a while if you disagreed too much. Although I guess that after eight or ten years of talking about comma splices and peeking at girls' thighs and saying, "Yes, in that case the semicolon goes *inside* the quotation marks," a man should be forgiven almost any aberration. Besides, he was one of these in-

tellectual idealists; he got into the racket because he had
the idea that as a man with the eternal wonder of Literature to unveil to his students, he would somehow count for
something around campus. The fact that he didn't bothered
him, I think. Even the Aggie profs and the goddamn tennis
coach got paid more.

Finally it was all over—Giffling's little speeches, the endless stupid talk around the table with everybody laughing
their heads off every time Dancer or Manquero said something, the songs, the closing prayer, the endless shaking of
hands. Manquero thanked Giffling for the meal and then
came over to say good-by to me.

"Good luck on your novel," I said.

"Yeah," he said, "and good luck to you and all your
friends this season too."

The guys all insisted on walking to the rally with Dan.
One kid wanted to stay at the House and read, but Giffling
wouldn't have any of that, and they dragged him along too.
Manquero was just pulling away when we got outside. He
had a real English teacher's special, bad muffler and all.

The rally was always held on the wide lawn in front
of the Memorial Fountain, where a wooden stand was
erected for the occasion. When we arrived the band was
already up there playing a rousing medley of college songs.
It was getting dark, and the sun was setting right on
schedule behind the massed sprays of the fountain, which
had a huge fish spouting upright in the center, and six
little fish spouting more or less haphazardly around the
circumference. The whole thing was supposed to commemo-
rate alumni who died in World War I. On the night before
final exams students were supposed to come and throw
pennies in it for good luck.

Willie Plasby, dressed in red trousers and white
sweater like the other yell boys and girls, but pre-eminent
among them by virtue of his white megaphone, was run-

ning about screeching directions for the preparation of the
bonfire, which was supposed to be ignited the moment the
sun set. The big lawn was already packed, with two or
three thousand students milling around. A lot of them
brought junk to toss on the pile, which infuriated Willie,
who kept scolding them through his megaphone. He wanted
a neat, well-organized bonfire.

"Listen to that music," Giffling exulted as we arrived.
The whole gang walked Dan around the wooden stand, to
the spot where the team was supposed to congregate. He
mumbled good-by, shaking a dozen or so hands, and
thanked them for the meal and everything. Pug was standing around with a few guys from the squad, and they
really eyed us strangely. We looked like a TV posse de-
livering the bank robber. I got the Kappa Delt troupe moving away, and then went over to Dan and Pug, who were
talking. I smiled at Pug, as if to say, "See, I got him here."
He did not smile back. Probably he did not smile because
he hardly ever smiled, although I realized it might also be
because of what I hadn't been doing with Dancer, or even
what I had been doing with Caroline.

"Hi," I said, very cheerfully, full of zest and innocence.
He did not seem impressed one way or the other. I turned
to Dancer. "Remember, we'll see you after the rally."

Dancer nodded. Pug looked at me suspiciously, as if
maybe we were thinking of going out and running around
the night before a game, but I reassured him with a wink
from the eye Dancer couldn't see, letting him know I was
on the job, watching Dan every minute of the day and
night. He nodded. I left, feeling the moment was well
spent.

Coming around the stand into the crowd again, I blun-
dered upon the Kappa Delt horde. "Jack! Jack!" It was
Giffling, who spotted me trying to sneak by. "Come on—

we're gonna stay together and give them some House cheers." He had my sleeve before I could get away.

"I don't know any House cheers," I said. "I'm very busy right now, really. I'll try to drop back later." I pulled away and headed into the crowd.

"Jack!" he shouted after me. "Jack—maybe Dan would like to come to our dance tomorrow night . . . Jack—"

But I was free. I was right near the big pile of broken chairs and crates and stuff, and suddenly a tremendous WHOOSH! vibrated against me—I could really feel the force of it, a strong hot gust—and a brilliant yellow glare illuminated the faces, the lawn, the trees, even the buildings across the street, as the kerosene-soaked pile caught fire with one match, flipped, no doubt, by Willie Plasby. It was really hot, and I moved deeper into the crowd. Everybody cheered the bonfire, and Plasby and his crew were leaping and tumbling over each other in front of the flames. Then Plasby called for silence through his megaphone and started a cheer. Most of the kids cheered. They'd probably jump off a cliff if somebody with a white megaphone urged them, and everyone else was doing it. It was pretty ghastly, pushing through that mob of open-mouthed boys and girls, half of them with beanies or red ribbons in their hair, watching their faces in the light of the fire as they swayed back and forth with their arms over their heads and moaned in unison, "CHOOOOO—OOOOO— OOOOO—*CHOO!*" All this time the band kept on playing. The band director and the yell chief never got along; they were always accusing each other of stealing time and taking the best moments at the games for themselves, so when Willie started his cheer the band director just increased his tempo and volume.

I finally got out and went across the street to the chem building. Peggy was sitting on one of the two lions alongside the entrance. Campus tradition, which sometimes tended toward cuteness, insisted that the lions roared every time a virgin walked by. Peggy was sitting on the back of the right lion, her hands on top of one another on his mane, her legs crossed. She was wearing a bulky sweater and skirt, standard campus equipment, and with her white hair glinting in the light from the bonfire she looked like some kind of Scandinavian moon goddess riding a sea monster. She jumped down while I held her waist and we bumped pleasantly.

"I missed you so much last night," she said.

"*I* missed *you*," I said. We hugged and kissed around a bit. "Peggy, I've got a terrific favor to ask you."

"Sure."

"Somebody's sick on the paper, and I gotta write up some extra stories and stuff. It'll take about an hour—would you be a doll and stay here and watch everything that happens very carefully and take notes so I can write it up?"

"You mean they expect you to be down there doing that other man's work and here watching the rally at the same time?"

"There are different bosses involved. It's kind of complicated to explain. Will you do it?"

"Of course I will. Let me drive you downtown first. I'll be back in time for—"

"No. You might miss something. I'll get a ride. Stay up front, on the left, so I can find you." I gave her a little kiss. "You're a sweetheart," I said.

I was careful walking toward the house, making sure the street was clear and that none of the neighbors were peeking out any windows. I went up the path quickly and quietly, but not suspiciously so, and tapped on the door.

Caroline was wearing a white sheath dress with a jet pin, more dressed up than I had ever seen her. She was usually in a robe or a house dress when I came over. Her face was carefully made up and I could tell she had worked on her hair. She was really good-looking.

"I'm glad you made it," she said.

"I really can't stay. You haven't said anything to Pug, have you?"

"No. Come on in and sit down."

"Just for a minute." I sat on the couch. She sat next to me. Two gin and tonics stood on the coffee table, one of them half gone.

"If you hadn't come, I was going to drink them both myself. To spite everybody. I was going to get drunk." She laughed. She had already had a few.

"I don't really feel like drinking."

"Then I'll drink it." She started downing the rest of hers, trying to swallow it in one gulp.

"All right." I held her glass, pulled it gently from her lips. "I'll have one." I picked up the other glass and sipped a bit. "Why are you so dressed up?"

"To make you stay. To entice you."

"You know I'd love to stay—but I really have to get back. Besides, we should be more careful now."

"Why? *Let* him catch us—let him walk right in on us. I don't care." She finished her drink and turned around on the couch to put her head on my lap. She put her feet up on the back of the couch. Her dress slipped down along her thighs and she started playing with my necktie, twisting it around her fingers, then unbottoned my shirt and put her hand inside and started rubbing me.

"Really . . . we don't have any time," I said. "We have to talk about this thing."

"I don't want to talk."

"Last night you didn't want to do anything but talk."

"You know what I want to do tonight—?" She laughed and pulled my head down to whisper in my ear.

"We don't have time," I said.

"Yes, we do," she said, and whispered it again, a little louder. Her hands were all over me now.

"We've got to talk," I said.

"We'll talk after. Let's do it now. Right here—we don't even have to go upstairs."

"On the couch?"

"On the floor. Come on. Now."

Afterward, she insisted that I finish my drink before she'd talk, and then we were on the floor again, and then she made me another drink. I was really thirsty and didn't want to bother going for water, and so drank some of that too. She sat alongside me and put her head on my shoulder.

"Let's not start again," I said. "We've got to talk."

"I'm listening."

"I don't think we should do this any more—until we know for sure what he knows."

"What are you afraid of?"

"Just tell me now exactly what Pug said."

"About what?"

"About us. About knowing."

"He didn't really say anything. I mean, directly."

"What *did* he say?"

"Well, I just asked him why he was so late—you know, what he was doing all night. That's all, just a question. But he looked at me very funny, and then he wanted to know if I wanted an exact schedule of his comings and goings, so I'd know the exact minute to expect him back. He said if that'd make things easier for me, he'd do it."

"Is that all he said?"

"Well, no—but everything was more or less like that. Hinting, sort of—but he never comes right out and says things, and after a while you can tell by the way he looks what he's thinking. You don't believe me, do you? You think it's all my imagination."

"Pug's no dope. It wouldn't surprise me if he knew. He looked at me kind of funny tonight too."

"You saw him?"

"For a minute—at the rally. I think we ought to just kill it for a while. See what happens."

"Then I'll tell him."

"Christ, stop saying that!"

"I will. I don't care if he knows or not. If he's out digging up football players and watching those goddamn movies all the time, I can at least have some fun while he's gone. He said he'll be watching them again tonight—probably all night again. Why don't you come back after the rally?"

"Don't be crazy. If he does know, that'd be a perfect trap."

"I don't care," she insisted. "Come back."

"No."

"All right, then. I'll tell him. I'll wait up for him and tell him the minute he walks in. I'll point to the exact place on the carpet. Right there, I'll say. Right there."

I straightened up, bouncing her head off my shoulder and grabbed her arms. "Have you gone crazy?"

"If I want a little fun, I'm not going to let him stop me."

"Well, what about me? Where the hell do you think that's gonna get me?"

"He won't do anything. He doesn't care."

"Well, for Christ's sake, *I* care. Don't say anything."

"Then come back tonight."

"No."

"All right. I'll tell him."

I didn't say anything for a moment. I still held her arms, pinching them tight, but she didn't seem even aware of it. Her face was pretty loose now; the make-up had worn off and she hadn't put any more on, hadn't even bothered to button her dress all the way. I let go of her and stood up slowly. "The hell you are," I said.

"I am," she said. "I am."

I turned and walked out of the house, and she sat there without moving, without saying anything.

CHAPTER FOURTEEN

Going back, I took a short cut through some lawns and back yards and then down Peabody Street. Between Caroline and all that drinking I could feel a beautiful headache coming on. In front of me, the sky over the campus glowed a sickly orange. Pug was probably introducing the team; every minute or so there'd be a burst of shouting and applause, all sounding remarkably like what it was, a kind of mindless belching of pure noise.

The president's house was on Peabody, which hadn't even occurred to me when I decided to come this way, but as I crossed his driveway a pair of headlights came on, startling the hell out of me, and I had to hop out of the way as the black Oldsmobile Ninety-Eight purred down the slope. The big soft front tires touched the street and the car stopped, slanting forward, overlapping the sidewalk at both ends. Irvine leaned his head out the driver's window.

"Jack? That you?"

"Why, yes . . . yes, it is." I stepped closer. "I—I'm surprised you're not at the rally, sir." Along with his annual appearance at the Birds luncheon, he probably hated the rally as much as anything, but he always went.

"I'm surprised you're not," he said.

"Just had to leave for a minute—I'm heading back right now to cover it."

"Of course. We want everyone to read all about it tomorrow."

"They will, sir. Have no fears."

"And will my absence be noted in the public press?"

"Would you rather it wasn't, sir?"

"I don't see that it makes much difference, really. Whether or not I'm there, I mean—not whether you mention it. But if you do, please say that the president was prevented from coming by illness." He made a little noise in his throat, something like a laugh, but not really. At first I hadn't wanted to get too close to him with the gin on my breath, but I needn't have worried. He wasn't drunk, but he'd had a couple.

"Will you be able to make the game tomorrow, sir?"

"I—yes. Yes, you may write that the president expects to be sufficiently recovered to attend the game."

"It probably won't be necessary to go into detail, sir."

"As you see fit."

He waited now, looking up at me, his arm resting on the wheel, the motor muttering, the lights splashing down onto the pavement. We could hear the cheers, still coming in regular bursts, sometimes accompanied by a roll of drums.

"What happened with that kid?" Irvine asked. Maybe alcohol affected him the way it did me; he seemed awfully put out about something.

"Why . . . he died, sir. It was all in the paper this—"

"I know," he said impatiently. "I read all that. I want to know what happened."

"The story was pretty straight . . . except maybe for the quote from Dancer and everything. The kid hurt his head, but it didn't show up until the next day. I guess it happens like that sometimes."

"Yes. I guess it does."

We listened to another ruffling of drums and another cheer, a big one, the biggest so far. Maybe Pug. Or Dancer. The roar continued and got louder.

"And how do you feel about it, Jack?" he asked, raising his voice a little, but otherwise ignoring the noise.

"About the kid? I . . . I don't know, sir. But it wasn't Dancer's fault," I added quickly. "I was there; I saw the whole thing."

"I didn't ask whose fault it was. I asked you how you felt about it."

"Well, I feel bad, of course. Little kid like that. Really. But . . ." I shrugged and faded off. I wasn't going into any weeping and wailing act for Irvine. I'm glib enough in my own way, but how do you *tell* a person the way you feel about some kid dying? It was a stupid question.

But Irvine was in a lousy mood and was convinced I didn't feel anything. I could smell a lecture close by, or maybe a fatherly chat about the value and dignity of human life—this with me sweating to get back to the damn rally before it ended and Andy Rivers took off, which would mean I'd have to take the stories downtown myself, which would mean losing sight of Dancer, which would screw up everything. Besides, I wasn't in the mood for Insight and Understanding. I really wasn't.

But all he said was: "Pug feels bad. It's truly disturbed him. In some ways, I guess he thinks he was at fault."

"He wasn't, sir. It was nobody's fault. It was an accident."

"I'm not trying to blame anyone. I was just going to say that he went over to see the parents today, and I went with him. It was quite an experience . . . for all of us."

"Oh—I didn't know you people went. We probably ought to run a story about—"

"If you write that story," he said, pronouncing each word deliberately and emphatically, "I will personally cut off your right hand and feed the fingers to you piece by bloody dripping piece."

"Yes, sir."

He paused. He was really boiling. "Benny came with us too. He's a good friend of Mr. Rending, it seems, and he also feels very bad. Did you know that?"

"No, sir, I didn't." I was going to say I didn't particularly believe it, either—that last part, about Benny feeling bad —but decided not to.

"Benny fools you sometimes." He waited again. He had all the time in the world and saw no need to rush things. "A boob, yes, but he does a lot of good for the school."

"In addition to helping the team, sir?" It griped me to hear Irvine defending Benny. "That's all I've ever heard of him doing."

"Of course that's all you've heard of," he said in a real grouchy way as if I was to blame for everything, "It's all you people down at the paper are interested in, it's all the people who read the damn thing are interested in . . . But this Rending man, for instance—he's been very generous to us; it's a shame he had to be the one whose kid got it like that. Sure, he's one of the Birds, but he's a lot more too. This school would fold up tomorrow without people like Rending . . . even people like Benny. It's one of the lessons one learns eventually."

"If that's the case," I said, getting a little grouchy myself on top of my impatience to move on, and probably somewhat emboldened by the drinks, "if we need people like that to keep going, then maybe we ought to *let* it fold up."

"Sure, Jack, that's the solution. You've got it all figured out. Jack," he said, very slowly, very sure of himself, "I envy you your certainties; you are a very bright boy, and an absolute horse's ass."

He smiled and nodded formally in my direction.

"And now, you'll excuse me. I'm going for a drive, some air. For my illness."

And then he hit the pedal and lurched around into the street, those big soft tires squealing piercingly enough to make me wince.

"What the hell is going on?" I shouted at the goddamn muttering exhausts farting in my face. "What the hell is everybody jumping on *me* for?"

I ran most of the way back, because the cheers had stopped and I was sure someone had taken the trouble to arrange the whole thing so that everyone would be gone when I got there. Then as I came puffing up close enough to see that—through sheer carelessness, no doubt—the rally was still on, with the band getting ready to begin another number and a couple of majorettes flipping batons and kicking about in front of the wooden stand, I couldn't even feel good about it, because I was out of breath and my legs ached and my head was throbbing.

I found Peggy down front, sitting cross-legged on the grass. She was scribbling frantically and didn't even notice me come up.

"How'd it go?" I asked about as pleasantly as I could manage.

"My God, Jack, I've been writing like crazy the whole time! How do you ever manage to keep up with everything that goes on at these things?"

"You get used to it. Let's see what you have." I flipped through about ten pages of solid writing. "You're a regular news hawk."

"I don't know if you can read it all. Let me go over it."

"No, it'll be all right."

"Well, here—can you read this? It's from the minister's benediction. I'm not sure I got his whole name, but I did get most of his main points, I think. He was from some

Baptist church. He spoke awfully fast. First, he blessed the
University and the faculty and everything, and then he
asked God to help everybody with their studies so we
could beat the Russians and then he asked special guidance
for the young men—and this is a direct quote if you want
to use it—who were to perform on the manly fields of
athletic endeav—"

"That's fine," I said. "I can read everything."

"One more man's supposed to speak. A Mr. Johnson."

"I had hoped to miss that," I said.

But she was right. The band stopped and the majorettes
tiptoed off with their backsides wiggling and Benny—who
was sitting on the platform along with Pug and the minister and Andy Rivers and the whole football squad—came
forward to give his annual talk, his round, bald head glaring in the floodlights. The speech seemed a little longer
than usual, but otherwise about the same. It was pretty
hot on Americanism and democracy and everything, and
he must have reminded the audience about fifteen times
how proud he was to have carried the University's honor on
the field of glory in his youth, and sort of hinted how that
was probably why he was today as great an American as
he was.

"You don't find football players taking dope or growing
beards or playing around with Commie ideas," he said, the
microphone blasting his voice over the campus. "I bet you
couldn't find a single Commie on a single football squad
in the country—and I say thank God you can't, thank God
for the healthy American sport of football!"

(This from the great humanitarian and friend of education. I don't know, I thought: maybe I'm the one who's off
his rocker.)

When Benny finished, the band played another number
and then everybody sang the Alma Mater, and Willie
Plasby announced through his megaphone that they were

going to start a snake dance at the bonfire and everybody
was invited and they were going to snake-dance all across
campus, and then Benny leaped up and yelled into the
microphone: "Come on! Everybody! Let's go! I'll lead the
way!"

He jumped down from the platform and the band
started again and the crowd began pushing toward the bonfire.

"I'll see if I can get Andy to take this stuff down and
have somebody else write it up," I told Peggy. "Maybe he'll
give me a break with all that extra work I did."

"That'd be swell," she said. "Do you want to get in on
the snake dance?"

"Christ, no. We're gonna meet a couple of friends."

"I thought we were going to be alone."

"I promised these people. It's Dancer and some girl."

"Oh—he got the biggest hand of anybody tonight. Is
he a friend of yours?"

"Yes."

"They had a moment of silence for that little boy before."

"That must have been very nice. You wait here now.
I'll be right back."

I caught Andy coming off the stand and gave him the
story I had written up earlier.

"Pretty quick," he said. He always said something like
that, even though he knew I had to do the damn thing
ahead of time to make the deadline. I also gave him the
practice story.

"That should have been in earlier," he said, wiping his
brow.

"I couldn't get downtown. I was tied up. Do you want
me for anything in the morning?"

"No. I'll see you up in the box. Be there early."

"Yes, sir." I always worked the games in the press box

with Andy. I was supposed to assist him, taking notes and keeping statistics and stuff, but I usually ended up writing most of the story for him. He'd do a lead and a couple of paragraphs and tell me to fill in the rest.

He shoved the stories in his pocket and walked away. The squad was off the stand now and breaking up, and with all the students heading for the bonfire and Willie Plasby shouting through his megaphone and the band playing, everything seemed kind of chaotic. I was afraid I might miss Dan and started running around pretty wildly, but then I spotted May and saw that Dan was with her. I dropped Peggy's notes into a bush and went over.

"Hi," I said. "Had trouble finding you."

Dan nodded. "Hello," May said. She looked pretty good in a skirt and white blouse. Her face would have seemed a lot better if she unstarched it once in a while and smiled a bit. She sure didn't smile when I came up.

"Peggy's waiting," I said. "Let's pick her up."

They followed me, holding hands, through what was left of the crowd. It was sort of strange seeing Dan with a girl; he looked out of place with girls. The band was still going, and Plasby was hopping around in front of the bonfire, organizing the snake dance. I helped Peggy up from the grass and introduced everybody. May looked kind of plain and colorless next to Peggy. Platinum hair really stands out, especially at night.

"Did Mr. Rivers like what I did?"

"Oh, yes," I said. "He thought it was great."

"I didn't know we were all going out together," May said. Her voice was like her hair, brown and dull. Peggy always talked as if she was talking about the most exciting thing that ever happened to her, and her eyes were always popping and she was always jumping around. May just said what she had to say, as if the whole thing was a kind of duty.

"Dan and I thought it'd be fun," I said.

"Where are we going?" May asked.

"Since we shouldn't stay out late, maybe we could have a soda down at the Mezz and—"

"No," Dan said.

"All right," I said. "You name it."

"Maybe you two could go for a soda," May said.

"I thought it'd be nice if we stayed together."

May and Dan looked at each other. They were still holding hands. "Maybe we could go down to the Venice for a hamburger," May suggested.

"Fine," I said. "Whose car should we take?"

"Both," May said. "In case someone wants to leave early."

"Where are you parked?"

"Second and Cherry."

"We'll follow you over."

Peggy and I went to her car and drove to Second and Cherry.

"Why can't we just meet them there?"

"Because."

We waited until they got in, then followed them. May had a beat-up '53 Mercury, but she drove pretty fast. "Stay with them," I told Peggy.

"What a crowd," she said. "Only the girls have cars."

At a red light, she started playing around, kissing, and when the light changed May zoomed away. "Don't lose them," I said.

May must have thought, or hoped, she had gotten away, because instead of going to the Venice, she headed west on Pinckney Street, out past the hospital and onto the highway. But we managed to hang on.

"Gee, that poor kid," Peggy said when we passed the hospital. "I bet Dan feels just terrible."

"Yes," I said. "Everyone is taking it very badly."

We went past the cutoff to the reservoir and out to Bar-

ney's Bedlam. Barney's was a roadside tavern and dance
hall, about fifteen miles from town, and over the county
line, where the officials were more lenient about closing
time and serving minors and things like that. The kids
who wanted a couple of beers went to Smoky's in town; if
they really wanted to drink, they came out to Barney's.
We followed May into the parking lot.

"The Venice has redecorated," I said after we all got
out.

"We changed our minds along the way," May said. "We
didn't think you'd mind."

"Not at all."

The place was crowded. Friday was always a good night,
especially before a game, when a lot of the alums came
back and revisited the haunts of their wild youth. It took
about ten minutes before you could see anything inside
Barney's, and then all you could make out was the big
bar and the shuffleboard game and the jukebox, which was
silent because they had a combo on weekends. The combo
played in the other room, where booths and tables were
crowded around the dance floor, and where it was just as
dark as at the bar. I was glad; I didn't want too many
people seeing Dan, especially with me. Benny would have
loved that. Pug too.

We got a booth near the dance floor and waited for a
waitress. The combo made it pretty hard to talk, so we
didn't say much. I was sitting between May and Peggy in
one of those semicircular booths, and I used the darkness as
an excuse to stare at May sideways a bit. I couldn't see
much, but I stared anyhow. May really got me. Somehow
you wouldn't expect the YWCA type to be the one to introduce Dancer to knife fights with drunken soldiers and all-
night dates and places like Barney's Bedlam. The waitress
came over and May ordered a whiskey sour and Peggy
a pink lady. Dan ordered rye on the rocks. That was another

thing. May had sure been able to work wonders with this
boy.

"I don't want anything," I said. "A coke."

"Come on," Dan said. He was grouchy too. This was
turning into Let's Get Sore at Jack Night.

"That's all I want. I don't like liquor."

"Don't be a wet blanket," Peggy said.

"Bring him a rye too," Dan told the waitress.

The band took a break and it was fairly quiet, but still
we didn't talk much. You could feel everybody trying to
think of something to start a conversation with. The drinks
came and I offered a toast to success in the game, as a reminder to Dan that there was, after all, a game the next
day.

"Oh, yes," Peggy chimed in. "We all wish you the *very*
best of luck, Dan." I think she was a little taken with Dan;
he was probably the first hero she had ever met.

We all drank, and then sipped in sequence—each time
one person picked up his drink, all the others did too, for
the next five or ten minutes. And then Peggy—naturally—
asked Dan how he liked the rally.

Dan shrugged. "It was all right."

"Who was that man at the end?" she asked.

"A jerk," I said.

Dancer kind of grunted at this. Everybody on the team
hated Benny, but sometimes it irritated me—even though
I was just as bad myself—and I was tempted to tell Dancer
that it was all right feeling superior to old Benny and
everything, but that he paid the bills. I couldn't quite bring
myself to be as broad-minded about him as Irvine was, but
at least I admitted that he paid the bills.

"Don't you like him?" Peggy asked Dan. I was the one
who said he was a jerk, and Dan had just grunted, but
she asked Dan.

"He's lower than horse piss on the grass, like we used to say."

"That's vulgar," I said. I was always trying to give Dan a little polish. He was one of these guys who were very moral about girls, who disapproved of shorts and tight sweaters, and then he'd come out with something like that right in front of them.

"What do you mean, vulgar?" he wanted to know. "Why is it vulgar?" He had already finished his drink, and I guess that helped. No matter how much May had been pouring into him, he still couldn't be used to it; it'd only been a couple of weeks.

"It simply is," I said. "Social convention. We don't talk about things like that."

"Why? You ever know a horse that didn't piss?"

"I haven't known many horses."

"We knew a farmer that had one once, and you know what happened? He died. Healthy horses always piss."

"Forget it."

Dan sulked a bit, then ordered another round of drinks. Everyone was finished except me.

We were quiet again. After about five minutes, Peggy brightened suddenly and said, out of nowhere: "It's not really vulgar, I think, unless you're trying to say it so it's vulgar. If you just mean it in a—"

"Christ, forget it," I said. "Come on, let's dance."

The combo was back, and Peggy and I danced. Dan and May stayed at the table; I was sure of that because I kept an eye on them.

"If you keep playing up to Dan," I told Peggy, "maybe you can get him to lay you. Or is that vulgar?"

"I was just being nice to him."

"You're gonna get May jealous."

"I'm trying to get you jealous." She laughed and kissed my ear. Her leg kept slipping between my legs as we danced.

"I'm glad we brought our car," she said. "Remember what we passed on the way out?"

"Yes," I said. But I sure didn't feel much like it. You keep reading all the time about these guys who knock off three and four girls a night, but somehow Caroline had managed to surfeit me for one evening, and the drinks on top of that and worrying about Dan made the reservoir the last place I wanted to be. Especially with Caroline home boozing it up alone and thinking of ways to ruin me. I tried not to think about Caroline.

We danced until the combo quit for another break and then sat down. Peggy patted my knee under the table, to show me she really wasn't trying to make Dan. May and Dan were still holding hands. They hadn't let go since we arrived, but it wasn't until we were coming back from the dance floor and I was watching them as we walked up that it really hit me. I mean the way they were holding hands, the way they looked at each other. Somehow this had just never really occurred to me, but Dancer was in love. Really. Knowing Dancer the way I did, I probably should have guessed it, because he wasn't one to go playing around for what he could get—he wouldn't consider it ethical—but it never occurred to me that he was actually in love. It just never entered my mind.

Dan finished his second drink and ordered another. I didn't say anything because I didn't want to make things worse. Sometimes he was very sensitive about being told things. I noticed May was pulling his arm, making a face as he ordered. Maybe she was afraid that after having taught him she had perhaps taught him too well. But he shook her off and ordered anyhow, just for himself, because no one else was ready.

The whole time we had been at the table, May had not once, I think, looked at me. She held Dan's hand and faced toward him, her back at me, but now she turned, without letting go of Dan, and said, "I've heard such strange things from Dan about you. Are they all true?"

"Probably."

"You write for the paper, don't you?"

"Yes."

"And you tutor football players?"

"Yes."

"And you give away cigarettes?"

"Yes. Do you smoke?"

"No. And you have a straight A average?"

"Yes."

"You sound like a fascinating person."

"It's funny Dan talks so much about me. He hasn't told me a thing about you."

"I'm not very fascinating," she said. "Tell me, is it true you met Dan because you were his tutor?"

"Yes."

"You were paid to do it, weren't you? And you still are?"

"That's right."

"I see. Tell me, what's your ambition? What are you going to do with all those brains and all that knowledge when you get out of school?"

"I have no ambition."

"What are your ideals?"

"I have none." Everybody Ask Jack a Stupid Question Night.

"Don't you want to be rich? Or famous?"

"Perhaps rich."

"But you must want something more than just that."

"You know what I want? I want when I die for people not to be able to say about me, 'Although he was actually pretty unsuccessful in everything, he was certainly an industrious worker.' That's what I want. I'm not sure if it's an ideal or not, but that's what I want."

"Is that why you get all As? So people can't accuse you of getting a B?"

"Look, I'm not the really fascinating guy around here. You don't read about me in the paper. Let's find out about you, Dan—What are your ambitions? Your ideals? What are you going to do with yourself? Is is true you're going to be an accountant?—or was it an engineer? Tell us all about yourself."

Dan said nothing.

"Come on now. After all, there must be something interesting about you—what with all those stories in the paper and everything. Enough of this modesty, now—tell us, what *is* your ideal? In one crisp, clear, grammatical sentence, tell us what your real true honest-to-Betsy ideal is."

Dan finished his drink. The combo returned.

"Maybe we should all dance," Peggy suggested.

"Dancer doesn't dance," I said. "Ironic, eh? That is, unless May has taught him that too."

"No," Dan said. "You people dance."

Peggy whispered in my ear that I should invite May to dance, that it wasn't polite to ignore her. I think she wanted Dan to herself for a few minutes.

"My girl friend informs me that it's impolite not to ask you to dance," I said to May.

"I'd love to," she said. She detached herself from Dan and we left Peggy and her hero together. I took May's hand to lead her through the people. It was pretty limp, and when we danced she stayed about ten feet away. I pulled her close, gradually, but she pushed back and then I pulled her close again and she said, "No," and pushed back, and then I pulled her close again and she stayed. They were playing pretty slow music and I rather enjoyed holding her tight. She was built something like Peggy, only shorter, and she managed, even without putting her leg between mine, to make the thought of going off to the reservoir more exciting all of a sudden. Maybe the drinks were beginning to work the other way now. Not that I liked her. But I would have liked taking her to the reservoir, just once.

Maybe she even felt the same way, because I didn't have to hold her tight any more. She never relaxed, though. She danced tensely, grimly, dutifully. And her hair had no smell—she was the first girl I ever danced with whose hair didn't smell of something besides hair.

"What are you trying to do to Dan?" she said.

"Keep you from ruining him. I've been teaching him English and history and chemistry. What have you been teaching him?"

"You're sore because you want him all to yourself," she said. "You're the one that's ruining him."

"He was doing all right with me before you came along. You don't want a boy friend, or even a lover—you want a kid, a baby, a fetus. Tell me, does he call you Mama? I mean, during those real intimate moments—is that what he calls you?"

I expected her to step back and haul off at me, the way I had expected her to do it that morning down at the Y, but she didn't, just as she hadn't then. She didn't say anything. She just kept dancing. And then she said, "I love Dan."

"And he loves you. Fine, fine—that excuses everything. That makes everything all right. But kids have been ruined by girls who love them, you know. Of course, I don't love Dan, so you've got me one-upped there, but I do kind of like the kid and wouldn't mind too much—especially, as you mentioned, since I'm being paid for it—helping him get through school, and I try not to do anything—anything—that would keep him from getting through. Like taking him out the night before a game for a few drinks, or keeping him up all night playing tiddly-winks or whatever it is you played last night until 7 A.M. He missed practice today, you know. If you really loved him so goddamn much, maybe you'd make a little effort tonight to get him home and into bed, his bed, alone. That guy represents quite an investment to the school, in case you haven't ever bothered to add everything up, and there's thirty-five thousand people who are not going to take well to him showing up tomorrow with a hangover. Did that ever occur to you? I realize the blinding force of love and everything, but—"

"It was his idea," she said. "Not mine."

"Cut it."

"Why don't *you* get him home? He idolizes you."

"Because he's not waiting to get me down on the grass."

She still didn't do anything, didn't even twitch. "It was his idea to come here, not mine."

"Sure," I said. "Big forceful Dan pushing meek little May around."

The music stopped and the dancers started moving off the floor, but May did not move.

"I thought maybe you'd help," she said. "I thought maybe together we could—"

"No thanks."

"But I can't do anything alone. If you don't help me, there's nothing—"

"Sorry, Mama, but we're on different teams. Let's go; the music's stopped."

On the way back to the table, she said, "I'll try to get him to leave."

"We'll follow you back," I said. "Try not to drive so fast."

"You don't have to worry. I'll take him home."

"We'll follow anyhow."

We returned to the table, where Peggy was going a mile a minute at poor Dan, who even in the darkness was beginning to show signs of the drinks. He did not seem to be listening to Peggy; he was watching us come up, watching May, looking at her with that sickly-drunk-in-love look of which only someone of Dan's limited intelligence and experience and his absolutely unlimited innocence is capable.

We sat down. It was after midnight. "Let's head on," I said. "I'm beat."

"Yes," May said. "It's getting late."

"I'm not tired," Dan said. He spoke to May, not to me. "Let them go home," he told her. He called the waitress over and ordered another drink. "C'mon, Jack—join me."

"No thanks."

"You've only had one all night. What's wrong with you?"

"I've had two. I don't want any."

"Bring him one too," he told the waitress.

Not only had I never seen Dancer drunk before, but I had never even seen him drink, and if I hadn't been so worried about people seeing us and about getting him home in one piece and onto the field tomorrow, I probably would have found his behavior interesting. He wasn't noisy; in fact, he didn't talk any more than he ever did. His silences were more sullen, though, and when he did speak his normal open-eyed sincerity was gone and he seemed fuzzily angry. He was also nervous, edgy. I thought maybe the old nightmare was hitting him again, the image of himself being carried off the field on a stretcher, dead or mutilated, and even thought maybe someone—maybe May —had told him that a couple of drinks would cure anything, and he was giving it a try. Only it didn't seem to be working.

"Wouldn't you really like to try to dance?" Peggy asked him. "It's really easy. Someone like you could learn in no time at all."

"I don't think so," Dan said.

"I'm quite good at teaching people to dance," Peggy said.

"I think we should go home," I said. "It's late."

"Don't be like that," Peggy said.

"All right," Dan said. "Let's try it."

Peggy took his hand and led him to the floor, and May and I watched them stumbling around. Dan was like a ballet dancer on the field, but he was unstable on the dance floor. Even Peggy, who was an awful good dancer, had trouble keeping him from knocking them both down. I guess the liquor helped, but being close to a strange girl probably had more to do with it.

Without even thinking, I was sipping away at my drink. You can never get a glass of water in a place like Barney's. You keep asking the waitress to bring you a glass of water and she says she will and then goes off and you never see her again. They use all their water for making ice cubes.

"We weren't very successful," May said.

"Maybe he'll collapse and we can carry him home."

Dan looked ready to quit on his lessons. They had stopped dancing and Peggy was trying to get him to continue. It was kind of too bad because they really looked good together, the handsome athlete and the big blonde with the nice figure, like those old pictures of Joe DiMaggio and Marilyn Monroe. That is, if you didn't notice how uncomfortable Dan was. I was watching them when suddenly I became aware of somebody behind me, high over me, leaning over the back of the booth to bend down toward me, and in that instant I felt one of those ultimate chills inside me, right at my heart, a kind of freezing and emptying sensation at the same time. Before I could turn around, I went through complete and detailed explanations for Pug, Benny, Andy, even Irvine, with everything carefully reasoned and explained, everything accounted for—

"Have a Royal King! They're mild as a smile, gentle as a mountain breeze!"

"Mr. Davidson—"

"Just call me Bob. What are you doing out here in this hole?"

"Just having a drink," I said. I was so relieved, I was numb.

"Have one with me. Come on, bring your friend."

"I really can't. There's a bunch of us together and—"

"Tell you what, then," he said. He had his arm around my shoulder. He was dressed in the same gray suit he had on this morning, but he looked pretty sloppy. Those neat, trim salesman types always look bad when they're drunk. "Just come along by yourself for a minute, just one minute —I got someone here I know you're gonna want to meet."

"I can't leave my friend here alone," I said. But just then, naturally, Peggy and Dan came back.

"He chickened out," Peggy said.

"See," Davidson said. "She won't be alone." He took my arm and dragged me off.

"I'll be right back," I called. "Wait for me."

Davidson took me into the bar and brought me up to one of those little two-seater tables along the wall. He introduced me to a woman in a purple dress, with a square face and a huge mess of dark hair. Her dress was held up by a couple of spaghetti strings over her shoulders.

"This is Veronica," Davidson said, pushing me toward her. "Veronica, this is Jack—we owe the honor of our acquaintanceship to Jack."

"We oughta buy him a drink," Veronica said.

"No," I said. "Really . . ."

"Waiter!" Davidson yelled. He pushed me into his seat and kept his hand on my shoulder as he ordered, to make sure I wouldn't get up.

"Bob is just a wonderful person, isn't he?" Veronica said.

"Yes," I said.

"Are you friends or business acquaintances?"

"Both," I said.

Davidson pulled up another chair to the outside edge

and the waiter brought the drinks. Davidson toasted their beautiful friendship, which they owed to me, and we all drank. I didn't even ask what mine was. All liquor tastes the same.

"Well, thanks a lot," I said. "I guess I ought to be getting back now."

"Not until you finish your drink!"

I drank the rest of whatever the hell it was in two gulps and got up, coughing. "It's been swell meeting you," I told Veronica, my eyes watering. "You're both wonderful." I shook Davidson's hand. "Thanks a lot, Mr. Davidson."

"Bob," he reminded me, holding up his finger. He gave me a cigar and laughed.

"Yes," I said. "Bob." I gave him a feeble high sign with the cigar. He winked, patting Veronica's limp hand on the table, and motioned with his head toward her cleavage. "Yes," I said. "Fine. Good luck."

"Onward, the queens!" he shouted after me.

I hurried out of the bar and across the dance floor. Peggy was alone at the table, looking bored.

"Hey—where are they?"

"They left."

"For Christ's sake, what'd you let them go for?"

"What do you mean, what'd I let them go for? I'm not supposed—"

"Run outside and hold them up. Hurry! Waitress! Where the hell's the goddamn waitress?"

Peggy started arguing with me, but I hustled her out and finally got the waitress. Dan had paid their half, which I guess is better than not paying it, but at the moment even that griped me. They couldn't just run out; they had to be gentlemanly about it.

I ran out to the parking lot, a little wobbly in the knees. Peggy was waiting for me in the front seat of her

car. She was powdering her nose and studying the effect in
the rear-view mirror.

"I could have told you they were gone," she said.

"Did they say where they were going?"

"Of course not. And I didn't ask. What do you care where
they're going? They're in love."

"You're breaking my heart," I said. "Leave me alone."

"What's the matter?"

"Just leave me alone."

Only she wouldn't. She wanted to go to the reservoir.

"Not tonight," I pleaded as she drove along the highway.
"I'm tired. I don't feel well. I drank too much. Besides,
your old man'll get sore if you stay out late."

"I told him I'm staying over with a friend in a sorority."

"All right," I said. "But first let's drive in to school, okay?
Just for a minute; then we can come right back."

"No. You just want to check up on Dan. Leave him alone,
for heaven's sake."

"You don't understand."

"I don't think it's very nice to use me as your lousy
chauffeur so you can run around after him all night. If you
want to go in, you can walk."

"All right," I said. "All right." I had her pull over to the
side of the road and sort of made up to her. "You've just
gotten me irritable by playing up to Dan all night," I explained. "I was jealous."

"I was just being nice to the poor boy. He seemed so un-
happy."

We kissed and fooled around a bit on the seat, but it
wasn't much of a place to stay, what with headlights going
by all the time and the chance of the state police spotting
us. We drove off, and I suggested once more, carefully,
that maybe we could ride in to the campus first, but again

she said she wouldn't, although not so angrily this time. She just seemed hurt.

"Don't you want to go to the reservoir with me?"

I didn't, naturally, but just as naturally I didn't say that, although I guess I should have. Something direct and honest, like: "No, I haven't the slightest interest in going to the reservoir with you tonight." But I never can bring myself to say things like that to people. Especially to someone like Peggy, who was basically a nice kid.

So we went. We cut off the highway onto the dirt road and then off that dirt road onto the one which took us to the other side of the reservoir, where no one would bother us. Only tonight, to keep my lucky streak intact, a car was there, with a couple blanketed down next to it. At first I thought it was Dan and May, but it wasn't.

"We'd better go somewhere else," Peggy said.

"I don't know any other place."

"Let's just follow the road a little more."

"Maybe we ought to turn around and go back," I said. The motion of the car over the dirt road hadn't helped my stomach.

"Don't be an old maid," she said. "This is fun. We don't even know where we'll end up."

We didn't know even after we got there. We found a little clearing behind a clump of trees off the road and pulled into it. When I got out to get the blanket from the trunk I realized how woozy I was. I was a little sick to my stomach, too, but there was no restraining Peggy.

"Ouch!"

"What's the matter, Jack?"

"Nothing."

"You poor boy—did I hurt you?"

"I'm all right."

"I'm sorry."

"It's all right. I'm fine."

I had a hell of a time upholding my end of things, but Peggy's enthusiasm carried the day, and when it was all over I got sick. I stayed in the bushes about fifteen minutes while Peggy waited on the blanket.

"I didn't realize you were really sick," she said, all solicitude, when I dragged back.

"I'm better now," I said. I wanted to rest a bit on the blanket, in the air, but the minute I lay down I realized I was falling asleep and made myself get up. "Let's go back. I'll be okay."

We turned the car around and headed for the other dirt road, but couldn't find it. We drove for about a half hour, and then thought maybe we had missed it in the darkness and turned around and went back along the same road, and this time couldn't even find the spot we had stopped at. We kept driving and came to a fork and took the right one. We drove on that for a while but it dribbled off into a little foot trail and so we turned around again and went back and took the left fork. We got stuck driving across a stream that flowed over the road and I had to get out and stand in the water, which was up to just below my knees and kind of slimy on the bottom, shoving forward and lifting up on the rear bumper until I was sure I could feel something rupturing inside me, while Peggy spun the back wheels so as to spray the rest of me more effectively with muddy water and sharp little rocks. Finally we got out, and after driving for another hour miraculously found ourselves out on the highway again, only far past Barney's, about twenty-five miles from town. The sky over the hills was turning light blue. It was six o'clock.

"Isn't that beautiful?" Peggy said. "Let's have some breakfast, okay? I'm starved."

"All right." I didn't feel much better than I had earlier, but at least I was drying out, and I was getting a little hungry. The riding made me awfully sleepy; I was really exhausted, I guess, much as I hated to admit it, and in spite of myself dozed off on the seat. I woke up with a fright when Peggy stopped at a highway café outside town. I hadn't even realized I was asleep; my mind seemed to be going the whole time.

At any rate, breakfast was a mistake, because the eggs started my stomach twitching ominously once more. The *Standard* was out, and Peggy bought a copy to see her story.

"Oh . . . they hardly used anything I turned in."

"That's the way it goes," I told her. I didn't even bother to read the thing. "Sometimes you write up a whole story and they just throw it away or change it all around."

"That's mean," she said.

It was light when she dropped me off at Ape Hall. There were even a few people wandering about. Peggy looked beat out but happy as hell.

"Let me wait and drive you to the House. I can't go home yet anyhow."

"No, I may be a while. Have another breakfast or something." I kissed her and got out. My shoes and socks were still wet.

"I haven't had such fun in years," she said. "I'm awful sorry you got sick."

"I'll be all right."

"Give me a ring as soon as you can."

"As soon as things settle down," I said.

"Watch out for Dad, though. Hey, why does he keep calling you a kike now?"

"I don't know," I said. "He must be a bigot." I turned to head off, but then turned back again. "Listen," I said. "Will you do me a favor? Will you just tell me what the hell you see in me?"

It just came out like that; it had been a bad day, a bad

night, twenty-four straight miserable hours. I guess I must
have been at the end of my tether.

"Beside the blanketing down," I added quickly.

"You're fun," she said with one of those shrugging smiles.
"You're nice."

"I'm not nice. Ninety-six per cent of just about everybody thinks I'm a horse's ass. It's a landslide."

"I know," she said helpfully. "Daddy does too."

"You don't even know how *old* I am, for Christ's sake!"

"You're overtired, poor boy, and you've got mud all over
your nice suit. What you need is a good night's sleep."

"I need more than that," I said.

I went upstairs and let myself in Dan's room without
bothering to knock. I knew it would be empty, but wanted
to make sure. Good old May, with all her talk about working together to help Dan. But I was too tired to be angry.
I couldn't even think well. Everything disgusted me, including myself. And then, while I was standing there trying to
decide what to do, I had to race down the hall in my
squelching shoes to take care of my breakfast. I came back
and flopped on Dan's bed and fell dead asleep.

CHAPTER FIFTEEN

The sun woke me, slanting from the window into my face. I lay a long time staring into it. I could not comprehend where I was, could not remember anything. Gradually I became aware of my head. At first it felt only dull and thick, but then the pain sharpened, pulsing like a shock wave across my head, right behind my forehead, from one temple to the other, and the longer I lay the worse it got, but still I did not move. My mouth was dry; my stomach empty and aching. I sat up and turned from the sun and rubbed my eyes. I realized by this time I was in Dan's room, in Dan's bed. The realization disturbed me, but only in a vague way. I moved stiffly to the dresser and leaned forward, holding on, to look at myself in the mirror. I sure was filthy, and my clothes were polka-dotted with encrusted mud. Inside my still damp shoes, I could feel my socks clinging to my toes. It was a quarter to ten. After staring at my reflection for a while, I walked cautiously down the hall to the washroom. Things were forming slowly. I washed, brushed what I could from my suit, and scrubbed the mud off my shoes with some wadded-up paper towels. A commotion outside drew me to the window. A gang of sorority girls with their skirts blowing in the breeze were parading a BEAT TECH! banner. A five-piece fraternity band marched briskly behind, playing the U "Fight Song," while about a hundred freshmen brought up the rear, singing with great enthusiasm.

I went to the House first. Somehow I had the idea that maybe Dan had come back and seen me in his bed and had decided that since I was sleeping in his bed he'd go and sleep in mine. I knew it was kind of far-fetched, but I had it on my mind. At the House everyone was getting ready to go to the game and decorating the place for the dance. That meant mostly putting around all their stolen STOP and ONE WAY signs. I went upstairs without talking to anyone, waving them all away, and found my room, as I had expected, empty. A note on the door said Pug had called and wanted me to call him.

"When did this come?" I shouted down the stairs. "Who took the message?—Why the hell don't you guys sign these things, or put a time on them or something, for Christ's sake!"

No one knew anything about it, so I went along the hall banging doors. "Who took the goddamn message? Where are you?" Finally I found the guy. "When the hell did this come?"

"About an hour ago. What're you making such a racket for?"

"Next time put the time on," I said.

"He wanted you to call right away."

I went into my room and changed into clean clothes. As I was leaving, I met Giffling in the hall, heading toward my room.

"Not now," I said.

"It's very important."

"I'm busy." I pulled my sleeve away.

"Wait a minute, Jack. It's nothing wrong—it's about to-night."

"I don't know if I can make it."

"We were wondering if you could let us have some cigarettes—you know, to put around and everything. That's all."

I went back into the room while he stood watching me and bent over and dug into the closet and started throwing cartons of Lords back at him, hiking them between my legs like a center, flipping them around my legs with both hands, flinging them at him so fast that he had to dodge and back up.

"Really—I don't think we need this many . . ."

"Here!—Have some! Have some more! All you want!"

I emptied out the whole goddamn closet and then puddle-jumped over the cartons and went out, leaving Giffling staring down at them, a little stunned.

"You got a message before," he called after me. "From Pug."

"Thanks," I said.

"Don't forget to invite Dan for tonight—!"

I got some toast and coffee at the drugstore around the corner and carried it into the phone booth.

"I'd like to speak to Miss May Steiner."

"I'll ring her." I waited, eating, and then the woman said: "Miss Steiner does not answer."

"Does that mean she's not in?"

"I'm sure she would answer if she were there."

"Was she in at all last night? Did she come home?"

"Who is this, please?"

"Her incubus."

"Who?"

"That's German for uncle. When she comes back tell her her German uncle called. This is very important—can't you tell me if she came back last night?"

"No, I can't."

"Aren't they supposed to be in by a certain time or any-

thing? What kind of a place do you have there anyhow?
Do you let young girls go running around all night without even knowing where—"

"Who *is* this?"

"Nobody. Forget it."

I went out and got some more toast and a glass of milk. I
really felt miserable. I counted up all the drinks I had had
during that twenty-four hour stretch, starting with Davidson and his portable bar in the morning, when I still had
a hangover from the night before. Seven, possibly eight,
possibly even nine. I wasn't sure. But more than I usually
drank in a month. And with three hours' sleep. I was glad
it wasn't me that had to play football.

I called the paper and asked for the news desk. I had
all kinds of premonitions.

"*Standard* news—Don Ames."

"This is Jack. What are you doing in the news room?"

"Filling in. What are you doing? Checking up on me?"

"Look, you had any accidents since about midnight?"

"A couple. No fatals, unfortunately. Very dull."

"Where were they?"

"Hell, I don't know. Wait a minute . . . here—farm truck
out on 103, and a couple from Iowa on 92."

"That all?"

"Yeah. Why?"

"I'm working on the side for an ambulance chaser.
Thanks."

"Sure. Say, Ace, Daddy Pooh-Bear was frothing over you
before. More than usual, I mean. Hold on."

I waited while he switched my call. I never thought
Andy would be there so early.

"Jack—how terrible! I'm heartbroken. Why didn't you
tell me you went blind and lost your sense of hearing like
that? I could've fixed you up for relief or something."

"What's the matter?"

"The matter is that so-called story you wrote last night—or last week, or last year. Look, all right if you work it up a bit beforehand, but maybe you oughta try to go to these things once in a while, too, and kind of see what happens there. Heh? You had people speaking who didn't speak, and people who did speak not speaking, and you didn't have anyone saying what they said, and you didn't even mention the goddamn minute of silence for the kid. What the hell were you doing there anyhow?—diddling with your girl friend?"

"Nobody will notice it," I said.

"Sure, like that baseball game, heh? Look, you're supposed to be a reporter, you know. Facts, you know. You ever hear of facts? I'm not paying you to be Hans Christian Andersen."

"I had to rush with the deadline and everything."

"All right—rush. Only don't make it up a week ahead of time. I'm gonna check last year's story, and, boy, if you turned in the same stuff last night you turned in last year, you can just—"

"It's not the same as last year's," I said. It wasn't. I made it all up fresh.

"We'll see. Get to the game on time. And call Pug—he's been trying to get you all morning."

"Yes, sir. Good-by, sir."

I was going to check Dan's room again, so that if he were there I could tell Pug everything was fine, but I was afraid if he wasn't there it'd be too late in the morning to tell Pug I didn't know where he was. I should have called Pug as soon as I got his note. That was stupid.

Anyhow, I called him from the booth in the drugstore, trying his office first, hoping he'd be there so I wouldn't have to call his home and take a chance on getting Caroline.

Pug answered and I asked him if he was looking for me.

"Yes, as a matter of fact, I am," he said. Very quietly. "Where've you been? Where are you?"

"Why? What's up?"

"That's what I want to know. That's what you're being paid to know so you can let me know when I want to know. Where's Dan?"

"Sleeping, I guess. I just got up and haven't had a chance to—"

"At eleven o'clock in the morning? Where the hell was he last night that he has to sleep until eleven o'clock in the morning? Besides, he's not in his room. I called."

"Maybe he's out having breakfast. Or taking a walk. A lot of times he takes walks before a game."

"You should *know* where he is. What do you do, sit on him all week and lose him on Saturday? What time did he get to sleep last night? I saw you two there with those girls."

"He went to bed early. Very early. We just went out for a coke. He got a good night's sleep—that's probably why he was out so early this morning."

"Well, I want you to find him. Find him right away, and then let me know you've found him, and then stay with him. He's supposed to report at twelve-thirty, and when he reports I want you walking alongside him, holding his hand."

"What are you so worried about? He's not going any-where. He'll be there."

"Was what I said clear?"

"Yes, sir. Very clear."

"I'll be waiting to hear from you."

I left the drugstore and tried to hitch a quick ride to Ape Hall, but the pregame traffic was a mess and nobody would pick me up. Christ, I couldn't even get myself a lift any more. Everything was magnificently under control.

I didn't knock, because I didn't want to wake Dan if he

was in bed. He would need whatever sleep he could get. Opening the door with my key, quietly, delicately, I was rewarded for my pains by the sight of an empty bed. But it was mussed, and for an instant I had a flickering of hope. Then it came back that I was the one who had mussed it and left the mud stains, not Dan.

I called May again from the phone in the dorm, but she still wasn't in.

"Is this her Nincumbus again?"

"Yes," I said. "It's very important. If she comes in, have her call Main 2-7845."

"Whom should she ask for?"

"Her uncle."

I walked to the House. Maybe they had gotten stuck out in the woods somewhere and had called in to let me know. I hurried up the stairs and almost lost my breath when I saw two pieces of paper tacked to my door. While covering, rather rapidly, the remaining fifteen feet of hallway, I decided that I was willing, if one of them was from Dan, to let the other be anything it wanted.

The first said:

Mr. Johnson called. Call his office. AP 5-1195

And the second, in a different handwriting:

Coach Walters wife called—very important—story—says come over right away, *not call*—Extremely important.

Didn't anybody in town have anything to do on Saturday mornings except call me? Oh, yes—two people, who were evidently so busy doing God knows what that they didn't have a second to spare.

I dialed Benny.

"Jackie boy—" he shouted. "That you?"

"Unfortunately."

"What?"

"Nothing. Yes, it's me, sir."

"Good. You know what I'm calling about?"

I thought of several prime possibilities. "No, sir."

"Well, it's about that story you did. A real great job—I just wanted to tell you so."

"Story, sir? What story?"

"About that kid dying. I know Andy had his own fat name on it, but Sam Rending's an old buddy, and he told me it was you out at the hospital that night getting the story. Anyway, it was a damn decent job, and I was glad to see the poor kid, rest his soul, at least get that much. Sam appreciated it too. Whole thing was just terrible, makes a man sick."

"Yes, sir . . . Well, I'm glad you liked the story."

"I did. And when I like something, I like to say so."

"That's very fine, sir. I . . . I heard some nice things about you too recently."

He seemed skeptical. "Oh? What'd you hear?"

"About how much you've been helping the school."

"From who?"

"President Irvine."

"Uh-huh. I can just imagine what that son of a bitch had to say. But never mind him. Tell me," he said, lowering his voice, "how's Dancer taking it? About the kid, I mean. Pretty bad, heh?"

"Well, yes—of course, sir. But he realizes it was an accident."

"Sure. Wasn't nobody's fault. And I thought that was damn white of Sam to say so in the paper. Shows the kind of man Sam Rending is."

"Yes, sir."

"Anyhow, Dancer's all set for the game?"

"Raring to go."

"Good. Good. You know what?—I think we're gonna win today, Jackie boy."

"I sure hope so, sir."

"And remember, Benny knows who's doing what around here. Don't think for a minute that I'll forget your part in all this."

"Thank you, sir. That's very reassuring."

Rereading the message from Caroline, I was tempted to throw it away and pretend I never got it. But there wasn't anything I could do to find Dan that I hadn't already done, and it hardly paid to knock myself out trying to keep Dan from ruining me in his way while leaving Caroline free to ruin me in hers. I tried again to get a ride, but it was hopeless, and by the time I got there it was eleven-thirty. I strolled right up the path without trying to be inconspicuous or anything—what the hell, it was the middle of the day.

Caroline came to the door in the same white dress she had on the night before. She still had not fixed her make-up or her hair. The dress was buttoned up now, though. The surprising thing was that she still looked good, beautiful, although now there was a kind of desperation in the endless movement of her eyes.

"Come on in."

I went into the living room. "Why couldn't I just call? I'm very busy this morning. There's a game on and I have—"

"Christ, don't you start that too," she said. She sat in the armchair.

I remained standing. "Are you drinking already?"

"Still."

"You ought to go to bed and get some sleep. You'll feel better."

"Will you stop it? You sound like an echo." She went into the kitchen and came back with a drink.

I sat on the couch. At least she didn't bring anything for me. "When did Pug get home?"

"I don't know. Five o'clock. Six o'clock. Something like that."

"And you waited up for him?"

"Yes."

"It must have been a pretty long night."

"It was."

"And you told him?"

"I started to."

"But then you didn't?"

"No, I didn't."

"I figured you wouldn't."

"I tried to. I would have, but he never gave me a chance." She was almost finished with her drink. She kept shaking it, staring at the ice cubes, listening to them. She sat with her legs crossed and her white dress spread out. She had not put her stockings back on. They were still on the chair where she had dropped them last night.

"I don't follow," I said.

"Give me a chance."

"I really have a lot of things to take care of and—"

"Oh, shut up." She kicked her legs apart and went into the kitchen. I waited. She returned with two drinks.

"I don't want one."

"It'll get rid of your grouch."

"I don't want it."

"I'll drink it myself then."

"Go ahead. Only tell me what you want to tell me."

"We had a big fight."

"You and Pug?"

"Yes. He started it. The minute he walked in the door he was sore as hell and he just started going at it. That's why I didn't get a chance to say anything. He just started in."

"Maybe he noticed something—the glasses—something. There's enough around . . ."

"He didn't say anything."

"What was he sore about?"

"I don't know. Everything. He was just sore."

"He must have been sore at something. Maybe he was just tired. He's been working hard and—"

She laughed. Out loud, rocking back and forth in the armchair, swinging her legs up as she went back, laughing as loud as she could. I waited for her to stop.

"Sure," she said. "Working real hard. Only you know what he's been working on?—some secretary in the Home Economics department."

For a few minutes I was quiet. She finished her drink and started on mine. I hadn't touched it.

"Did he tell you this?"

"Yes—he just came right out and told me, before I even had a chance to say anything."

"Why did he tell you?"

"I told you. Because he was sore at me. He just got sore and started shouting and everything and then he told me. Maybe he didn't even want to tell me, I don't know. But he told me—in all that shouting and everything suddenly he was telling me. Can you imagine that? Some goddamn secretary in the Home Economics department? And here all the time we're feeling sorry for poor Pug down there working out plays and watching movies and all that crap and he's out somewhere getting laid."

"And you never got around to telling him about us?"

"No. He left."

"Still sore—only what was he sore about?"

"I don't know."

"Yes, you do." I went into the kitchen and brought back the gin bottle. There was maybe an inch left. I put it down on the coffee table, feeling like somebody in a movie—not very satisfied with myself or anything, but conscious of my-

self, as if I were sitting in a theater watching myself on
the screen.

She stared at it. "It wasn't all the way full."

"I thought it was."

She shrugged. "What the hell do you expect?—you and
Pug both. Sure, you got places to go all the time, both of
you. You got this to do and that to do, but I know what the
hell you do. You go out and get what you can, wherever
you can, secretaries, nymphos, college students—I bet
there's some real good stuff around in the dorms. I'm surprised Pug hasn't discovered them yet. And meanwhile I'm
supposed to stay home and read a good book. Improve my
mind. Sure. That's what he used to say, you know: 'Why
don't you read or something while I'm gone?' He figured
that'd be a lot of fun for me, great sport. Because he was
very busy, you see. Christ, we hadn't been married two
weeks when he had to go off somewhere to some damn
conference or other, or visit some high school or something.
You can't even talk to him, you know—I mean about anything besides football, and half the time he won't even talk
about that. He just thinks about it, twenty-four hours a
day, morning, noon and night."

"Even when he's with his friend from Home Economics?"

Her eyes stopped. She stared at me. "Maybe you ought
to ask *him* about that," she said, a little quieter now.

"When'd you start drinking?"

"When you came over."

"I don't mean this bottle. I mean the first one."

"I don't see anything wrong with having a drink. Christ,
all I ever do is sit around here anyhow."

"But Pug knows . . ."

"What do you mean, Pug knows? Of course he knows.
Why shouldn't he? I'm not doing anything wrong. I
haven't got anything to hide."

I got up from the couch. "I've got to go," I said.

She shrugged.

I waited a moment. "Is this the first time for Pug?"

"It's the first time he's told me."

"But is it the first time?"

"Yes."

"And for you?"

"Just go to hell," she said.

I started out, but stopped at the door. "You know, he won't even believe you now if you tell him."

"He'll believe me. He—" She didn't go on.

"He knows," I said. "Sure. He's known all along, for the last two or three or four years, or whatever it's been, and for the last two or three or four guys. He just doesn't really care who they are, does he? He's just glad there's someone to take you off his hands so—"

She got up from the chair and turned hard on her heel and headed for the kitchen.

"The bottle's on the table," I said.

It was almost noon; the traffic was hardly moving as I hustled toward Ape Hall. I couldn't decide whether I felt sorrier for Caroline or Pug. I was going to tell her that I didn't give a damn what she said, or what she said Pug said, but that Pug wasn't stabbing any Home Ec secretary. He had his faults, but they were all all neatly circumscribed by the noose Benny and the Birds were dangling casually around his neck. His whole life was circumscribed by that noose—which, by the by, good old dependable Jack Wyant hadn't been doing too much to loosen of late. Anyhow, that was what had pulled out the plug for Caroline, not any secretary. She probably wished it *was* a secretary. Something human. Christ, no wonder, she hit the bottle. They were really a pair, him with his pills and her with her gin. Why the hell did people have to get themselves all full of pain and nervousness and meanness and everything?

Why couldn't they just go along and let life alone, and let it let them alone?

Although when I got to Ape I was about ready for a few pills or something myself. Dan still wasn't there.

"Hey—Jack!" Chuck Janowski called from his room as I hurried past down the hall. I didn't know exactly where I was hurrying to, but I just didn't feel comfortable standing still. I came back and looked in his doorway. Some of the other guys were there with him, sitting around, smoking cigarettes; one guy was drinking a glass of milk. They already had their white shirts and ties on. Pug made everyone come to the games in a suit and tie. You could really feel the pregame mood, because no one in the dorm was shouting or horsing around the way they usually were, and considering how noisy it was out on the campus, the whole building was pretty quiet. The guys in the room were very still, their faces set, sober, a little drained. Football players were the greatest kidders in the world, the greatest jokers, but they knew better than anyone else on campus that business is business, and Saturday morning they were all businesslike.

"Where's Dan?" Chuck asked with what was supposed to be a casual shrug. The other guys were watching me.

"Around," I said. "Have you seen him?" I sounded about as casual as he did.

"Can't say I have."

"He likes taking walks before games," I said.

"It's getting kind of late."

"He'll be there. You guys are just a little nervous."

A couple of them shrugged. Chuck got up and nodded for me to go out in the hall. We moved away from his door. He leaned over me confidentially, his great square face vacantly somber: "Dan was out last night, you know."

"Oh?"

"Yeah. We had a couple of beers ourselves and I felt

pretty good so I went down and knocked on his door when we got back. I thought maybe he'd like to—"

"No use a lot of people knowing about it."

"I ain't said nothing. I just thought maybe you knew where he was."

"I'll check around. Don't worry; he'll show up."

I went downstairs and called May again but she still wasn't in. I started for the House. My head hurt and I was pretty tired from all that racing around. When I was about a block from the House I saw the beat-up '53 Mercury parked in front and ran the rest of the way. May was sitting on the couch in the living room, alone.

She got up when I came in and we stood for a moment looking at each other. There were a few guys around, fussing for the party, and they all stopped to watch us.

"Hello," she said. She was still wearing the dark skirt and blouse she had on last night. She looked all right, though, and seemed to have come through the night a good deal better than either Peggy or Caroline. Her eyes were clear, her brown hair was combed, her face was made up, that tight face that always looked as if she were hanging grimly onto something. But this time some of the tightness was gone. Her eyes seemed softer, quieter, her mouth fuller.

"Hello," I said. I didn't ask where Dan was. I almost did but then decided not to, and took great satisfaction in my decision. "Won't you sit down?"

She looked at the couch behind her, then at the guys watching us.

"Rather go up to my room?"

"Can we?"

"This isn't the Y," I said. I led her upstairs. Actually, we weren't allowed to take girls above the ground floor, but no one paid much attention to the rule. I motioned her into

the room, and she sat on a chair. I closed the door and
sat on the bed.

"Haven't they ever seen a girl around here before?"

"They stare automatically. It's nice getting together
again."

"I'm returning the compliment of your visit the other
day."

"I'm flattered." For a few minutes neither of us said anything. I had decided I wasn't going to ask her, and she had
decided she was going to wait until I did. It's stupid getting
in holes like that, but I had spent the whole goddamn
morning grinding my legs down looking for Dan and trying
to speak to May, and now that I had her it seemed to me
I shouldn't have to be forced to ask.

May looked around the room, at the bed and at the shoes
under the bed, at the neckties hanging from the mirror, at
the typing table, at all the junk on the dresser, at the
clothes in the open closet. There was even a carton of
Lords on the floor that Giffling must have overlooked.

"I've never been in a fellow's room before," she said.

"You've led a very sheltered life." Although as I said it
I realized I had never had a girl there before. It was a small
room, and seemed much smaller with a girl in it.

"I guess so." She was quiet again, but not looking around
any more, waiting, and when she saw I wasn't going to say
anything, she said. "I almost came to see you earlier."

"Why didn't you?"

"I promised not to."

"Who'd you promise?"

"Dan." She paused, and then said: "He's gone."

"To the stadium? Good. Be just on time. Pug likes his
boys to be on time."

"No. Gone."

"Not to the stadium?"

"No." She looked down at her feet; they were moving on

the floor under her chair, shifting position. She had narrow
feet, fragile looking ankles. "I was going to come and tell
you at seven o'clock, when I got back, but I promised I
wouldn't. I've been sitting on a bench in front of the library
downtown all this time."

"Was it just a five-hour promise? I mean, is it all right to
tell me now? I don't want you breaking any trust or—"

"I just promised I wouldn't tell you right away. He's going home."

"Home?"

"Back to Humbolt."

"It's a long walk."

"He's hitchhiking. That was funny—I tried to talk him
out of that, into taking a plane or train or something, but he
wanted to hitchhike."

"He likes hitchhiking," I said. I was taking it all very
calmly. I just wasn't excited, wasn't even worried any more.
We were just sitting around talking about something that
had happened a week ago a thousand miles away, to someone I didn't know, hadn't even heard of.

"I wonder how far he is now," she said. "That's why I
wanted to come earlier, so we could go after him—so you
could go after him—before he got too far."

"Go after him?"

"Yes. Bring him back. I fought myself all morning on
that, whether I ought to come right over and tell you or
not. You know why I didn't? Because of you, because I
knew just what you'd say—that Mama had promised him
something but felt she didn't have to live up to it because
she knew better, because she was doing it for his own good,
and then I decided not to come."

"Do you want him to come back?"

"Of course."

"You're kidding."

"No."

"When did he start?"

"As soon as it got light. I waited around the bend until I saw him get a ride. It was right after you went by."

"It was what . . . ?"

"Right after you two drove by. We were still in the car then and I guess Peggy didn't notice us. You were on her shoulder."

I didn't say anything. But it was what I should have expected. All Jack Wyant has to do is close his eyes for five lousy minutes . . .

"Were you asleep?"

"Asleep? Me? No. I never sleep, didn't you know that? I can't afford it. But never mind that—what I want to know is why didn't you go too? Why didn't you both go in your car?"

"Go where?"

"To Humbolt. To wherever the hell you wanted to go."

"I said no."

"Did he ask you to go?"

"Yes."

"Directly? Did he say, 'Will you come too?'"

"Yes."

"And you turned him down?"

"I wanted him to stay here. I talked to him for hours, trying to make him stay; I talked to him until the sun came up and then he just said, 'No,' and got out and stood by the side of the road and waited for a ride."

"Without even a suitcase, any clothes? Without anything?"

"Yes."

"What's he going to do in Humbolt?"

"Get a job."

"You mean he's just going to sit around in that goddamn town for the rest of his life?"

"No. He's going back to school. Not this school, but some school, somewhere."

"And not play football?"

"That's right. Not play football, just study, and work if he has to, to make money to put himself through."

"What about his old man's car? What about his sister and brother's scholarship? What's he going to do, tell them all to go to hell?"

"He's going to explain it to them."

"He's got more courage than I have."

"I know."

"And what about you in all this?"

"I'll go with him. Maybe we'll get married after a while, but I'd go where he was anyhow and get a job and live in the Y or something."

"It's too late to start at another school this year."

"He knows. He's going to study this year. Read books. Try to get ready for next year."

"And you encouraged him? You told him he could do it? Could get himself ready?"

"Yes."

"He can't."

"He wants to try."

"But he can't do it."

"He deserves a chance to try. If he can't learn anything from doing it, maybe at least he can from trying. He knows what he's getting into. And if he goes somewhere next year and flunks out, that'll be all right too. At least he'll have tried, on his own. There won't be anyone pushing him through or pulling him through or faking him through just to keep him in uniform."

"Fine, fine—but how could you have encouraged him in this when you say you almost came to me this morning to stop him?"

"Because I don't think he has to go to Humbolt to get

away from Pug, or from you. I think he could have stayed
and told you both to leave him alone and just quit the
team. But he didn't think so. He thought he had to go
away, go back. We're not even going to see each other for
a year this way. That was all his idea. He feels it's the only
way he can do it, can come back to me, can tell you and
Pug to go to hell—by going back by himself to Humbolt
and staying there all year working somewhere and reading
all the time, studying every night, getting ready. And then
he said we could pick out a school, pick it together and
go off to it, and maybe get married or maybe wait a while.
But he wouldn't do it any other way. He wanted that
year."

"But you said he asked you to come?"

"He felt he had to. He was being polite."

"And you said no?"

"Yes."

"But you really wanted to?"

"Yes."

"Why can't you tell this story straight?"

"Because sometimes you ask me what he said and sometimes you ask me what he wanted or what he thought."

"When did he decide he wanted to go? When did all
this start?"

"He's been ready to go ever since he got back. I thought
you knew. He didn't even want to come back this year in
the first place. Pug had to go there this summer and talk
him into coming back; he spent three days there, in Humbolt, talking to him and his parents before he could get
him to come back."

"No wonder Pug was worried."

"I thought you knew. I've been fighting with him day by
day to keep him here. He would have gone two weeks ago
if I hadn't stopped him. He would have gone last night, or
the night before, or the night before that. Every night we

fought it out, and last night he won. He even mailed the
letter he's had all written up for weeks now . . . to Pug."

"I bet it was a masterpiece. What did he say?"

"Only that it wasn't because of him, of Pug. That he
liked him. It was the money, really. All that money. I think
maybe if they had only given him less money, a lot less,
just enough to get by, or to not quite get by, and made a
lot less fuss about him, he wouldn't have felt so bad. He
really felt bad about all that money."

"Maybe he was just afraid to play. Maybe that's why
he left."

"No."

"Yes. He was really scared. He had nightmares."

"I know. But that wasn't it. And it wasn't that little kid
dying either. He was sure everyone would think he left because of the little kid. He felt bad enough about it, but
that wasn't why he left."

I got up from the chair. "I should call Pug. Maybe we
could still find him, get him back in time for the game. The
cops on the highway could—"

"All right. But it has to be you, not me. I couldn't let
him think it was me."

"But it's all right if he thinks it's me?"

"Of course. He'd expect you to do it."

"But I thought you didn't want him to play football?"

"I don't care if he plays or not. But I want him to stay
here. I don't want him off there for a year."

"Christ," I said, "if he loved you so goddamn much, why
couldn't you keep him here?"

"He was ashamed."

"Ashamed?"

"Yes. Isn't that something? He was just ashamed, of himself, of everything. And you were so worried about me
twisting him around my finger. I couldn't do a thing with

him. He's like a stone wall when he makes up his mind. Go ahead," she said. "What are you waiting for? Call Pug."

"Ashamed?"

"Yes. Ashamed."

She was standing now, right in front of me, looking up at me, her breasts pushing against that wrinkled blouse that she had worn last night and had been wearing all this morning and that had probably been unbuttoned and re-buttoned a few times along the way—and finally I just figured, *The hell with it, I've had it, I don't care.* Who knows, maybe it was that inverted bowl of brown hair, those dull brown eyes, that dull dull brown face and voice. At any rate, there it was, and so I said to her, very simply and pleasantly and for once in my life without a single disguise or despicable motive: "You are a beautiful girl and I love you." I meant it of course in a very noble and broth-erly way, but I was sincere—sincere!—as I was sure she would realize as I stepped forward to plant upon her fore-head, right below the brown bangs that smelled of nothing but brown bangs, a most chaste and brotherly kiss.

CHAPTER SIXTEEN

It was two-twenty; the kickoff would be at two-thirty. The teams had warmed up, doing calisthenics, racing up and down the field, kicking, passing, calling signals, their new bright red and bright blue uniforms like satin in the sun, their big white numerals glistening, and now were back in their dressing rooms for a little water, for the tightening of a shoulder-pad lace or the adjustment of a helmet strap, for a few minutes of relaxation during which no one would relax, for a few final words from the coach that, at least in Pug's case, would simply be directions, instructions, ending with nothing more than a quiet, "Good luck, men; we're counting on you."

It was a beautiful afternoon, what Andy Rivers would refer to as perfect football weather in tomorrow's page one story. The University had a long tradition of beautiful afternoons for opening games, with a strong clear autumn sun that had just enough summer left in it to mask the chill in the air. From the press box, which looked something like an elongated wooden matchbox glued to the top of the grandstand wall, the grass below always looked darkly thick and green between the regular white stripes, and the flags on the standards around the stadium fluttered at eye level, and when you looked out and away you could see pretty much all of Midland, trees and tops of houses mostly, and a few six- or seven-story buildings downtown. Andy Rivers had his chair in the center, smack on the fifty-yard line, and I always worked in a little smaller and less comfortable chair on his left, close enough to hear him breathing as I worked, to see his white handkerchief moving fitfully as I handled the lineup charts and the play-by-play sheets. It was a big press box, about thirty yards long, because the games were always covered by the wire services and all the big city newspapers in the state, and were usually broadcast by at least three or four stations, including the local one.

As I lay on my bunk, I could picture perfectly the scene in the press box, in the stadium. I could see the bands marching up and down in their pregame show, could see the stands filling in below the box, the townspeople and the alumni with their cokes in paper cups into which they poured whatever it was they had in their pint bottles or their flasks, with their wives wearing chrysanthemums on their fur coats and waving pennants. And across the way from the press box I could see Willie Plasby and his yell leaders leaping on the grass, doing cartwheels, dancing, clapping their hands, could see the cheering section, the card section spelling out FLY BIRDS, FLY, the square empty space for the band, which was now probably forming in front of the stands for the National Anthem. And I could hear the crowd, too, no one shouting now, everyone waiting, talking, with the talking of thirty-five thousand people sending up from the huge oval tremendous vibrating waves of rumbling noise, but of low pitch, low intensity, for this moment right before the teams returned from their dressing rooms would be one of the quietest of the afternoon at the stadium. And I could see Andy, wheezing and puffing asthmatically, perhaps sweating a little more than usual, could hear him fuming and cursing, wondering what the hell he was going to do with all the lineup charts and play-by-play sheets that I always very efficiently took care of for him, and maybe even wondering a bit where the hell I was.

It was getting close to two-thirty. I lay in my room, surrounded by the perfect silence of the House. Everyone else had gone to the game. Even the campus outside was quiet, and I did not have the radio on. I did not want to listen to the game, did not even want to think about it, but knew anyhow that I would see it all as clearly in my mind, almost down to the individual plays, as if I had been there, and that I would know at the end everything I would know if I had been there, except the score, except the outcome of the few key plays that turned the game to one team or the other.

I had called Pug. I had called right away, even with the pain, as soon as the agony had eased enough to let me stand and keep my balance, to let me limp along the hall, holding on, groping, to the phone, where I stood on one foot leaning against the wall while I spoke.

Pug was very calm. "Gone where?" he asked quietly. "Has he left town?"

"I don't think so. I don't know where he'd go if he did, or how. I think he's around somewhere, probably hiding."

"I see," Pug said. He didn't even sound surprised. "I don't know—are you sure? Maybe something's happened to him."

"No. He's gone. His girl told me."

"Does she know where he is?"

"No."

"You mean she says she doesn't know."

"No. She wants to find him too. I'm awfully sorry about this, Pug. Really. I—"

"That's all right. When did you see him last?"

"Last night."

"When last night?"

"Fairly early."

"Before midnight?"

"Oh, yes. Sure."

"Okay. I just wanted to know so I can tell Benny what time to stop paying you at."

I had hobbled back along the hall and lay down in bed again when I finished talking to Pug. I was glad he hadn't made a big fuss. I guess he knew it was coming, had known all along, especially since those three days he spent in Pennsylvania this summer. I guess he even knew it when he hired me, or when he got Benny to hire me. He figured it was just part of the breaks of the game, that some went your way and some didn't, and that he had tried his best and that this time the breaks had simply gone against him, although I'm sure he wasn't looking forward to next week's meeting of the Townbirds. But there were other halfbacks, other kids from other places who'd be glad to take a few thousand dollars a year to come to a fine university and play a little football and get the opportunity to meet thirty or forty other guys of similar backgrounds and interests. It was just Pug's misfortune this year, out of all those guys from all those towns like Humbolt, Pennsylvania, to get a guy like Dancer. And then I guess maybe Pug figured that it might not be too bad, after all, because he had a pretty solid team this year and might still be able to do well enough to keep Andy and Benny and the ravenous Birds off his back for another year—and Irvine too, if Manquero was right. I hoped he would, I really did. I also hoped that he'd be able to find someone to take Caroline and her beautiful long legs off his back. Someone else. I figured I had served him long enough in that capacity, especially since I didn't have much taste for gin.

There were two reasons, I guess, why I didn't tell Pug about Dancer being out on the highway somewhere.

In the first place, it wouldn't have done me a whole lot of good. Even if they could find him and get him back on time, that is—which they possibly could, since hitchhiking can be a pretty slow way of traveling. But Pug wouldn't have been any less sore, or Benny, or Andy, or even Irvine, for that matter, especially after they all learned about Dan and me out boozing it up together at Barney's.

But the real reason I didn't tell Pug was that I knew May was wrong, and Dancer right. He couldn't just come back and not play football. He had to get away altogether if he wanted to get away at all. And even though—despite all my faith in a person's ability to control what people like to call his destiny—I doubted that a year spent trying to figure out the jokes in *Huckleberry Finn* would really do for him what he wanted it to do, I kind of liked the idea of letting him try. You never could tell; Ezekiel saw the wheel; grass grows through pavement—maybe Dancer could learn to read.

As for myself, I didn't mind losing my grip on Benny's well-laden wallet. And I didn't even mind too much the thought of Pug deciding—on the basis of my having screwed up so ingeniously with Dancer—that he didn't want me tutoring his boys any more. Or even of Andy Rivers deciding to fire me again for my assorted sins, including having lost him his All-American and not showing up at the box today. Of course, I could always blame Dan's running away on May (a delicious irony: she's the one Benny should have been paying to keep him around), and could plead my injury in not making it to the stadium, but I wasn't sure I'd do either. I didn't need all these things; I'd get by. And I was almost looking forward to having Andy fire me and Pug and Benny boot me off the gravy train. All of it was just part of letting Dan go, and I figured

if I was going to let him go, I might just as well let him
go real good. Christ—ashamed! Ashamed of himself! That's
what really got me, that was the real kick, because I guess
all along, even when I more or less believed him about
wanting to learn and everything, I wasn't really believing
him. So I let him go, let him get good and far away before
Pug or Benny or Andy even knew what direction he was
moving in. I figured it was the least I could do, and in some
ways I kind of enjoyed doing it.

The pain was easing a bit now. I lay on the bunk with
my clothes on but my shoes off, on my back, my knees
up. It was the most comfortable position I could manage.
I wondered where May had gone, what she was doing. I
couldn't get any picture of her in my mind, the way I
could of Andy up in the press box, and Pug in the locker
room, and even Dan out there on the road, heading toward the same mountains he had come out of not too long
ago. But I could still feel it, not just the pain, but the kick
itself, the knee. I could still feel the electric shock. I had
never been kicked like that before, had never been hurt
there, not even in all those years of playing on that rock-
filled triangular gully we called a football field, and when
it happened and I was writhing on the floor with my knees
up, all I could think of was the other guys I had seen it
happen to, and how funny they had looked, and how much
worse it actually felt than I ever thought it did watching
them rolling around like clowns.

By the time I had opened my eyes and stopped thrash-
ing about, I saw that May was gone. She hadn't even stayed
to see if I was really hurt. But I didn't care; it was all right.
It was even kind of funny in a way. The Story of Jack
Wyant: His Experience with Chaste Kissing and What
Befell Him Afterward. But she would be perfect for Dan,
the way girls like Peggy were perfect for me. Not necessarily only Peggy, but girls like her, ones who don't have

any great ideals worked up ahead of time for their men, and don't expect anything too complicated or heroic from them. May demanded a lot, and was willing to give a lot in return. She'd wait for Dan, in a way that I wouldn't even *want* a girl to wait for me. She'd wait not only for the year it'd take Dan to unravel *Huckleberry Finn,* but even, if he wanted her to, for the five years, ten years, he'd need to meditate upon the whiteness of the whale in *Moby Dick.* And she'd be faithful, and pure, and full of hope. They belonged together, they were two of a kind, and I was willing, even without the poignant reminder she had presented me in the approved YWCA manner, to admit that somehow I never quite understood the kind of thinking people like that did. I could even believe now that they *had* spent all night arguing about him leaving or staying, sitting there on the front seat of her beat-up Mercury and holding hands and occasionally, perhaps, exchanging pecks upon the cheek. Although maybe I couldn't even understand them enough to realize how little I understood them; for all I knew, they might have argued the night away lying stark naked on a blanket in the grass. If May had just hung around long enough for me to get off the floor and get my breath back, I think that's what I would have asked her. I wouldn't have been sore or anything, although I guess she figured I would have. But I wouldn't. I would have just asked her what the hell they did all night during lulls in the great debate, because somehow I felt if I at least knew that, then maybe I could understand a few other things about them too.

It was two-thirty. The teams were out of their dressing rooms, with their sharp white numbers flashing on their red uniforms, their blue uniforms, and thirty-five thousand people were standing with their hats off and their hands, moist from their waxed Coca-Cola cups, on their left breasts, and the band was beginning its weekly butchering of "The Star Spangled Banner." The image was clear enough, but it kept fading out on me, and all I could see was Dan, standing alongside the road somewhere in the afternoon sunlight, without even a suitcase, and in a suit and shirt he had worn all night and had possibly even wrestled around on the grass a little bit in, too, but still looking like one of G.E.'s most promising executive trainees, and with this guy in a car pulling over and pushing the door open and Dancer getting in and closing the door behind him and saying in that bright, crisp voice of his: "Thanks." I could see the other guy, sort of middle aged, maybe a little fat, bald, saying: "Sure. Don't mind the game on the radio, do you?" And Dancer sitting back nice and comfortable on the seat, quiet, relaxed, saying: "Not at all." I could see him just sitting there, his hands in his lap, looking out the window to where the road twisted up through the green and brown hills and off into the mountains toward Humbolt, Pennsylvania, and all in all feeling pretty goddamn good about things.